This book is a work of fiction. Any resemblance to persons, living or dead, or places, events or locations is purely coincidental. The characters are all productions of the author's imagination. Please note that this work is intended only for adults over the age of 18.

S0-AGG-464

DAMAGED

R.R. Banks

Chapter One

Charlotte

Is this actually happening?

I stared out of the window of the car at the trees that were sweeping past as we bumped and bounced our way through the dips in a road that had taken a decidedly disheartening shift from smoothly paved to uneven gravel to worn dirt. The woods around me looked like it had to be teeming with starving artists ready to burst out from behind the trees and hunker over their canvasses to paint the undeniably picturesque scene as quickly as they could before withering beneath the sheer weight of their artistic angst and the disappointment from their family. We continued on through the woods and suddenly the trees broke at the end of a curve, revealing the cabin that my parents had rented for our Thanksgiving celebration. The driver brought the car to a stop and I didn't bother to wait for him to open the door. I stared at the cabin incredulously as I stepped sideways out of the car and let the door remain open as I took a few steps forward.

There has to be a tiny old woman holding a massive turkey at a ridiculous angle around here somewhere, expecting the magic of the season and the admiration of her family to defy the physics that were making her presentation of their feast a potentially dangerous impossibility.

"Isn't it wonderful, Charlotte?" my mother said with a distinct trill in her voice.

I knew by that sound that she wasn't entirely convinced by the whole concept of the rented cabin, either. That was one of the things about her that no one who knew her for more than a few days could get around, likely because she didn't even realize that she did it. It was her tell. The higher that her voice got, and the wider that her eyes grew, the more she was either straight out lying or at least trying to convince the people around her of something. At this point it seemed that she was in full denial, but if an entire lifetime of knowing her had taught me anything, it was that she wouldn't let up her charade throughout the trip. She would go to her grave swearing that this was the best Thanksgiving that we had ever spent as a family. And, lord help us, she would fully expect us to agree with her.

"It's definitely something," I said.

"I think it's lovely," Mom said, her voice creeping up even higher.

"Explain to me again why you thought that we needed to come all the way up to the top of a mountain to celebrate Thanksgiving."

"Well, we aren't really at the top of the mountain," she said.

Of course not. Because that would just be ridiculous.

"All right. Then explain to me again why you thought we needed to come all the way up to almost the top of a mountain to celebrate Thanksgiving."

"Your father and I just thought that it would be nice to have a change of pace. It's so beautiful up here," she said, looking around the woods and trying her best not to shudder.

My mother was many things, but a nature-lover was certainly not one of them. The most in touch with the Earth that I think that I had ever seen her get was when she participated in stomping the divots back during a polo game. Come to think of it, even that was somewhat traumatizing, and I couldn't remember attending another game with her after that. Whatever her motivation for renting this cabin and bring us all up here for the week, it must be something serious. It wasn't that we didn't celebrate the holidays together. We were a family like any other. It was just that us celebrating Thanksgiving generally meant my sisters and their families all going to our parents' home and sitting at an almost comically long table to eat a feast prepared not by our mother or grandmother, but by members of our staff. In all honesty, they might as well be members of our family. Many of them have been with my family since well before even my oldest sister was born, so in a way I suppose that was almost traditional. That made it seem even stranger when at the beginning of November my mother and father suddenly announced that they had rented a quaint little cabin in the woods so that we could get away for the Thanksgiving holiday. It would be so much more personal, they assured us. So cozy. We would be able to focus so much more on each other and making memories.

These are all things that I would have liked, of course. I would have loved to think that we would spend the week bonding, laughing and enjoying each other's company. Unfortunately, there was not a doubt in my mind that there were other reasons why they had planned to bring us up here. I could only imagine the gears were turning in my mother's mind even as I walked up the drive towards the steps that led on to the wide porch of the cabin. There was a reason that we were here. Soon enough I would find out what it was.

I stared in awe at the porch as I climbed the steps. It was deep enough that even if there was a storm, we could stand at the door and watch it without being affected. To either side at the far end were what looked like hand-hewn rocking chairs. They looked almost like props. I'm sure that there were some people who would rent this cabin and immediately see the chairs as a wonderful place where they could relax and enjoy their time away. To me, however, I had a difficult time imagining a lifestyle, even during a holiday vacation, that was calm enough that I would ever contemplate curling up in a blanket in one of these rocking chairs with a cup of hot tea and gaze out over the beautifully changing fall foliage. Even when I was home, relaxation was something I had very rarely, if ever. I woke up in the morning, got ready, went to work, and kept myself busy every moment that I was there. When I returned home, I either continue to work or I spent time organizing and reorganizing, decorating and redecorating, trying to make the little house that I had recently moved in to feel like a home. I very rarely sat for longer than a few minutes. Sitting down meant my brain had a chance to wander, and that was something that I didn't want to let happen. I didn't want any room for the thoughts that would try to creep in.

I stepped up onto the porch and turned around to look out of the trees. They were truly breathtaking, and I had a flicker of guilt at the distrust and suspicion that had colored my view of this trip with my family. Maybe my parents really had noticed that all three of their children were now adults and they were eager to make some of those cozy, warm memories of the holidays that other families enjoyed. Maybe they even recognized that this holiday season might be harder for me and wanted to be there for me, to comfort me and try to make it as happy as they could. I wanted to believe that. I wanted to think that their focus of all that had happened over the last several months had turned away from what society thought, from what they perceived as public opinion, and instead turned toward me and how it all impacted me and my life.

"Let's go on inside, Charlotte." My mother said as she hurried up the path from the driveway to the steps. "I'd love to show you around. I chose the smallest bedroom for you. I figured that you wouldn't mind. You know that your sisters just need more space."

Well, damn. Never mind.

I wasn't really disappointed by the confirmation that my mother had more on her mind than a greeting card worthy setting for eating our turkey. There wasn't any malice in it. She didn't mean to hurt me. I knew that. But that didn't change the frustration that I felt coursing through me as I let out a deep sigh and stepped through the door of the cabin. I figured that I had two choices. Either I could do my best to smile my way through the week and deflect all of the comments about my woefully single state so that I had some hope of a holiday that was worth remembering with my family, or I could take off running through the woods and hope that I made it down the mountain. I figured that the latter wasn't the most practical choice, so I took a breath and let my mother give me a tour of the cabin.

"You know," she said, as we walked through the living room and toward the kitchen. "This is the very cabin that Dr. Smith rented for his 30th anniversary party. When your father and I were thinking about this trip, I remembered how beautiful it was and knew that I wanted this particular cabin." She sighed. "I felt so lucky that it was still available."

I looked around. Dr. Smith was one of the wealthiest and most sophisticated people that I knew. I had a difficult time imagining him in this setting, especially having a party here. The cabin was lovely, I had to admit. But it was a cabin, in every sense of the word. Every room seemed to be a study in muted colors and whittled wood. With every turn I was worried that I was going to come face-to-face with the head of some unfortunate previous inhabitant of the woods. I wondered if there was some sort of themed element to the party that my mother was just not mentioning.

We continued through the house, my mother gesturing toward various features like she was displaying the grand prize on a gameshow and me giving little sounds of acknowledgment as we went, until we reached a tiny bedroom tucked in the corner of the lower floor. I could only imagine that this had once been a nursery or even servants' quarters. My luggage was already sitting there waiting for me and I plastered a smile on my face as I turned to look at my mother.

"Thanks, Mom," I said with as much enthusiasm as I could muster. "This is going to be great."

The truth was, it actually could be great. As different as this holiday season was going to be, I was looking forward to the opportunity to spend time with my parents and my sisters without distractions.

"Madeline and Miranda should be here soon. I hear that there is some exciting news!"

She was grinning at me again as if she had no idea what the news could possibly be, but if I was to take my guess, there wasn't going to be any real surprise in the news that was coming. Both of my sisters had done exactly as was expected of them and went to college with more of an intention of getting their MRS than any other assortment of letters, and within weeks of graduation both were dutifully wed and on their way to starting families.

"I look forward to seeing them. I should probably get started unpacking."

I opened my suitcase and was surprised to see my mother step up beside the bed and reach in for one of the shirts that I had carefully rolled and tucked inside. She unrolled it and shook it, carrying it over to the closet to hang it almost as if this was a normal activity for her. I doubted that she had done her own laundry more than a handful of times in her life. Violet was very secure in her place as a member of high society, a position that she fulfilled with a level of enthusiasm that belied the fact that up until her father got very fortunate and very rich, she lived a firmly middle-class lifestyle. That was something she never talked about and preferred if everyone pretended didn't exist. It might tarnish her reputation if people started acknowledging that she was among the newest of the new rich.

"You know, Charlotte, your father and I were really hoping that this Thanksgiving we'd be able to celebrate your marriage."

And there it is.

"Please, Mom," I said, dropping my hands onto the top of the clothes still in my luggage and looking at her pleadingly. "Please, don't."

"Please don't what?" she asked, innocent as though she really had no idea what I was talking about.

"We've already talked about this. It's been months since Daniel and I broke up, and that's it. It's over. I know that you really like him, but..."

"We *loved* him," Violet emphasized. "He was wonderful."

"Don't you think that it should be more important whether or not I loved him?" I asked.

"You didn't?"

I sighed. This wasn't a conversation that I wanted to have. Not now. Not again.

"Can I just unpack, please? I'm here alone. We all know it. That's not going to change this week. Please, let's just try to enjoy Thanksgiving."

My mother finished hanging up the shirt that should have gone in the drawer with the pajama pants that it matched and nodded.

"I'll just go downstairs and get supper started." She walked to the door, then paused just before leaving. "Will you be coming down soon?"

I nodded, giving her a small smile.

"Sure. I'll just finish unpacking and I'll come down."

"Good."

She closed the door behind her as she left and as soon as I heard the click of the doorknob engaging, I stalked across the room to the closet, pulled down the shirt, and brought it back to my suitcase. I tried not to think about my mother's less-than-subtle prodding while I put away my clothes and changed into the stretch pants and oversized sweater that had become the source of my obsession as the cold weather crept in. The cabin smelled like the bold, rich spaghetti sauce that I knew was my parents' cook's family recipe. I could only imagine that she had packed up a few jars of it for Mom to bring along and heat up for us. I found her leaning over the open oven, staring into it in bewilderment.

"Are you looking for something in particular?" I asked.

She backed up and looked at me.

"I don't want to burn the garlic bread."

I laughed, remembering the one meal that my father had attempted to prepare for us when I was younger. It was one of three days during which the vacations of the kitchen staff all overlapped, and my mother was pregnant with my younger sister Madeline. She was craving Italian food and my father decided that it couldn't be but so challenging to make spaghetti. He boiled the pasta. He opened a store-bought jar of sauce and warmed it. He even opened a container of grated parmesan cheese. Things went fairly well, until he attempted to make the garlic bread. Rather than turning on the oven, he blasted the broiler, and within minutes the kitchen was full of black smoke and Dad was running through the back door holding a baking sheet with a flaming loaf as far ahead of him that he could. He had never tried to cook again and more than twenty years later Mom was still traumatized.

She suddenly grabbed an oven mitt and snatched the pan out of the oven. I peeked at it and smiled.

"It looks perfect."

She gave a relieved smile and I couldn't help but cross the kitchen and give her a squeeze around her shoulders. I kissed her cheek and picked up the bowl of pasta from the counter, following her into the small dining room. I had just set the pasta on the table when I heard the door to the cabin open. I turned and looked over my shoulder to see my older sister Miranda walk-in, quickly followed by her husband Seth, and her two young children. They were still going through the rounds of hugs and taking off coats when the door opened again, and Madeline and her husband William came in. Excitement swelled through the cabin as family who hadn't seen one another in months started to catch up. I could see a grin on Miranda's face, and knew that she was the one with the news that my mother had mentioned. That smile clung to her lips as we all settled down around the table and began to pass plates and cups. My mother accepted the plate that I held out to her and placed it in front of her before turning an almost giddy smile to Miranda.

"So... What's this big news that you were talking about?"

Miranda and Seth exchanged glances and then stood. He looped one arm around his wife's waist and held up a glass of champagne. Miranda mirrored his gesture, but with a glass that was conspicuously filled with the apple juice that had been purchased for the children.

"Well," she said, looking up adoringly at Seth. "We are going to be having another baby."

My mother gasped and clapped her hands together, her eyes sparkling with a joy that was almost enough to make it seem that she didn't predict the news. I smiled and started to stand, wanting to hug my sister, but before I had the opportunity, I noticed Madeline stand up. She, too, was holding a glass of apple juice and her cheeks were high with color. She smiled at each of us and then at William.

"Then I guess this may be the perfect time for us to make our little announcement," she said.

"Really?" My father asked, sounding nearly overcome with excitement.

"You, too?" My mother asked.

My little sister nodded, smiling so hard her blue eyes were nearly shut. Another round of hugs and kisses commenced with questions about due dates and morning sickness and birth plans and all manners of other things that I felt I had nothing to do with, taking over the dinner table conversation. I was thrilled for both of my sisters and content to sit back and watch their lives unfold in front of me. Both of them had taken the path that was expected of them, and neither looked like they could possibly be happier. I had taken another path, but I felt like I was making progress, taking steps towards finding a place in my life where I might find that type of happiness.

"So, Charlotte, when are you going to have news for us?"

All of the happiness and levity that had filled me from the moment that I saw my mother trying to prepare dinner drained out of my body. I felt cold and my stomach turned. I looked at my mother, incredulous that she would ask me that question.

"Didn't we just have this conversation?" I asked, fighting to keep my tone calm.

"Well, yes," she said, "but I thought that hearing your sisters' news would motivate you a little more."

"Motivate me?", looking between my parents and then to each of my sisters. "What's that supposed to mean? What is it supposed to motivate-me to do?"

"Maybe it should motivate you to grow up and have your own life," my mother said.

"I have my own life," I protested. "I did grow up. I live in my own house. I have my own career. I have my *own* life. Just because I don't have a husband and children that are a part of it, does not mean that my life is not my own. In fact, maybe that means that I have more of my own life than either of them do. Or that either one of you do."

I heard one of my sister's gasp, but I didn't turn to see which one. My father held his hand out over the table as if trying to create a barrier between me and my mother.

"Alright," he said, "maybe we should all just calm down. Violet, I thought we agreed that we would bring this up more delicately."

"Bring it up?" I asked. "So, I was right. You actually did plan this whole Thanksgiving week trip as some sort of bizarre intervention."

"Now, Charlotte, don't think of it that way."

"How else do you want me to think about it?" I glanced over at my sisters who were both leaned on their husbands, their hands rested protectively over their bellies in mirrored displays of maternal concern. I gestured at them. "You two are just mad that I didn't get married in time to be a part of the gestational hat-trick. Well, I'm very sorry that I ruined any plans for a triple baby shower. I'll make sure to keep everyone's social calendars in mind the next time I contemplate making decisions about my own life and own future."

I stepped away from the table and stalked down the hallway and into my tiny bedroom. I was nearly trembling with anger, but there were tears stinging in my eyes. This was exactly what I didn't want to deal with when my parents suggested we spend the holiday in this cabin. I was proud of how far I had come. I was proud of myself for pulling out of Daniel's clutches and finally claiming exactly what my parents thought that I didn't have: my own life. They claimed that they loved him, but they didn't know him. They didn't see the person that I did. They didn't understand what I went through with him every day. I had tried to tell them. So many times, I tried to find the right words, to explain to them the pain that I was in or the terror that I faced whenever I knew that I would see him at the end of a bad day. Even when I was able to tell my mother, she seemed to filter it out, as though she wasn't processing what I told her. Now that I was finally away from him, I looked back on those days and wondered what could have kept me there, what could have allowed me to let the years slip past.

I took a deep breath and squared my shoulders resolutely. This was the same thing. I was just continuing to give Daniel power over me, and I didn't want to give him another minute. I wiped the tears from my eyes and walked back into the living room. My family was talking in hushed tones and fell quiet as I approached. Their eyes turned to me and I paused just inside the doorway.

"I apologize for my behavior," I said. "It's the holidays and we shouldn't be fighting."

My father stood up and wrapped his arms around me for a hug, then guided me back to the table. I sat down, and we slipped back into our meal, all of us skilled at the art of glossing over unpleasant moments and moving on.

Chapter Two

Micah

I stayed inside long enough for the chill to leave me and to swallow down another cup of black coffee. It tasted like licking an ashtray, but it warmed me deep in my belly and kept me pushing through the long days. I had tried other types of coffee, looked for one that wasn't as harsh, but I didn't find it as satisfying and always ended up back with the bitter brew. The cold air outside had settled deep into my bones and ached in my leg, sending a sharp, intense pain through me that was as familiar as the smell of the wood burning in the stove. The stove pumped heat through the lodge, but it wouldn't take away the pain. Not yet. That would require a long soak in hot water and a few hours of rest, and that meant that the ache was going to be with me for quite a while. The sun was still high in the sky and that meant that I had to keep moving. There was still much too much to do to even think about the relaxation that only came at the end of the day.

I gave myself just a few more seconds, then pulled my thick gloves back on and stepped back outside. The temperature had dropped sharply from the day before, telling me that the forecasts that had been steadily streaming through the radio were accurate. Over the last couple of hours that forecast had shifted from just letting the inhabitants of the mountain know that the winter weather was on its way to warnings of a severe storm that would soon be bearing down. The people in the valley down below would experience cold temperatures and maybe some wind, but up here in the thick woods of the mountain the snow would soon be falling, and the temperatures would continue to drop unbearably low. That meant that I had a tremendous amount of work to do before even the first flurry made its appearance.

Gripping an axe in one hand and the leather strap of a sled in the other, I started away from the clearing that surrounded my lodge and into the woods. Scout burst out of the treeline and rushed toward me, his eyes shining and his mouth open, tongue flapping around his face. He seemed thrilled by the cold, as though he could feel the anticipation of the fierce weather that was on its way. He was like a little child getting excited for the first snow of the year while completely oblivious to any dangers that it might present.

"There you are," I said, reaching down to pat the dog's thick black and white fur. "I wondered where you got yourself off to. Did the squirrels want to play with you today?"

He looked up at me as if to complain that they didn't. I loved my dog, but a hunting companion he would never be. He would much rather romp through the trees trying to engage the squirrels, rabbits, and other little animals in rousing games of tag than try to take down a deer or even carry home fowl. Not that I hunted very often. In fact, I hadn't actually gone into the woods on a hunt in a couple of years. There were plenty of aspects of self-sufficiency that I readily accepted and even relished, but hunting down my own food turned out to not be one of them. I would rather source my meat from the providers closer to the base of the mountain and know that my freezers were full before the cold weather hit. That might make me lose a bit of my mountain cred, but frankly it was only Scout there to judge me, and he thought that I was pretty impressive even without chasing animals around hoping for a burger.

I made my way into the woods and found the downed trees that I had been working on. I made sure that Scout was a safe distance out of the way and went to work chopping the massive trees into smaller pieces and stacking those pieces on the sled. I secured them in place as I went, making sure that I fit as much on to the sled as I could without compromising the structural integrity. The last thing I needed when I was dragging it back to the house would be for the straps to break or one of the pieces to fall loose and let all of them tumble off the sled. That would only mean doing my work over again and expending more energy. My years on the mountain had taught me that when it came to preparing the lodge and the land around it for severe winter weather, every moment was important. Every bit of energy that I expended needed to be as useful and effective as possible. When the snow began to fall, and the wind began to whip through the trees and batter down on the lodge, I didn't want to feel that it was a morning that I slept in or an afternoon of work wasted that meant I wasn't prepared. I had already been working to prepare myself for the winter for several weeks and I felt confident that I would be ready when the storm began.

The axe swung over my head and I let out a grunt as the wedge of metal blade bit into the tree in front of me and split it. Soon the two halves were reduced to 8 smaller pieces that I would use to fuel my stove and to make fires in my fireplaces. They would keep the lodge warm and in the event the electricity went out, I would still be able to cook and melt down snow. This was a major part of why I enjoyed living on the mountain so much. Nature was the great equalizer. It didn't care who I was or had been. It didn't recognize my name or have any assumptions about me based on it. It didn't care how much money I had in the bank. The billions that I made in software were nothing when I was standing in the woods. When it came down to it, nature treated everyone the same. Either you put the work, the sweat, and the energy into preparing and protecting yourself, or you were at the mercy of the mountain.

Being out here working in the woods was also a good counterpart to the years that I had spent working in an office. Being outside and using my body this way spoke to a primal part of me, a part of me that I had not been able to indulge in those years. The work that I did in the city might have brought me my success and my wealth, but now that I was up on the mountain I felt that it was real life. Up here, I wasn't constantly bombarded by people and things were never just handed to me. I put everything of myself into my work or nature would prevail. It was that simple.

When I finished chopping as much wood as would fit on the sled, I secured it with the last of the leather straps, called to Scout, and started dragging the load toward the smokehouses. They had been billowing constantly for a couple of weeks now and the smell of the meat inside laced the cold, pine scented air. I reached into the first smokehouse and began cycling the meat, moving pieces from the hooks on the bottom up to the top so that each piece within the house would be smoked equally. I had been considering building a larger smokehouse that would allow me to smoke all of the meat for the season in one place, so I didn't have to attend to several fires or move the meat inside multiple different structures. Any construction on a new building, however, would have to wait until the spring and there was something to say for being able to use different wood for each of the different types of meat. Having gotten no closer to making a final decision about the smokehouses, I cut a chunk off of one of the pieces of meat from the final house and tossed it to Scout before securing the door and heading on toward the lodge with the remaining wood. This would be added to the growing pile that I kept easily accessible for my stove and fireplaces.

I was piling the wood in place when wisps of smoke across the mountain caught my eye. They seem to be coming from one of the cabins lower down on the opposite side of the mountain from my lodge. Those cabins didn't have full-time residents, but rather people who would rent them for a week or two at a time for vacation. Usually those people came in the spring and summer months to take advantage of the warmer weather and what they saw as a rustic experience. The cabins generally lay quiet and empty during the winter, with most people not interested in facing the potential of serious weather. This was so much the case that I sometimes forgot that the cabins were there at all. Now that I noticed that there was smoke streaming out of one of the ridiculously tall chimneys that protruded from the roof of the cabins, it seemed that I had neighbors for the Thanksgiving holiday, whether they realized that I was there or not.

The thought of the holiday brought a somber feeling. It had been many years since I had celebrated an actual Thanksgiving. Not since my mother's death had I had a feast or even really considered the day much different than the others around it. In the years before her death she would cook lavishly for both of us and we would spend the day together, ending the evening by putting up the Christmas tree. It always felt as though she were trying her hardest to make up for lost time, to make as many good memories as we could to cover up the ones that we wished we didn't have. After she died, I didn't see much point in continuing to go through the trouble of celebrating the holiday. Since moving up to the lodge I hadn't had any visitors and there was no one who I could think of who I would really want to share the holiday with, except for Scout. He was always there, right by my side, and I had to admit that he was one of the things in my life for which I was the most thankful. He didn't have the best table manners, however, so going through the effort of preparing a large meal to share with him wouldn't have much impact.

I was walking back into the house when the thoughts of my mother faded and were replaced by ones of Helen. My jaw set, and I willed my mind to push the image of her face away, but she seemed stuck there, unwilling to give me even a day's respite. I had gotten to the point when thoughts of her came less frequently, but they grew more intense during times when I imagined that we should have been together, like the holidays. I hated that she still had the hold on me that she did. It had been so long since we broke up and it seemed ridiculous that I couldn't put her behind me.

Broke up.

That made it sound so simple. So easy. Like the petty fights that teenagers have that result in the two of them getting back together or crawling in bed with new people within a week. That wasn't what Helen and I went through. I thought that she was going to be it for me. We had been together for years and she had been so happy to ride the wave of my popularity and success as my college football career soared. But then...

I shook away the thought, refusing to give her another minute of thought. She had already taken so much from me. She didn't deserve anything else.

My thoughts drifted back to Thanksgiving. I had the same plans for the day that I did every other year. I would work in the morning and then sit down to watch the football game, even though it tortured me to see it. I reached into the refrigerator and pulled out everything I needed to make a sandwich for lunch. Maybe this would be the year that I tried to have some semblance of a celebration. I knew that I had a chicken in the freezer. I could pull that out and let it thaw over the next couple of days. It wasn't quite a turkey, but roasted up with some vegetables and potatoes, it would be a more elaborate meal than I would usually sit down to and maybe it would give the day a bit more of a Thanksgiving feel. I didn't know why I was even thinking that way. It was as though there was something inside me telling me that this year needed to be different.

I built my sandwich on the kitchen counter and put it on a plate with a handful of potato chips and a large scoop of potato salad. My mother had always teased me for my taste in food. It was one of the few things about me that hadn't changed even after the injury, even after my focus in school changed. Even after the money started rolling in. I went into college eating like a teenage boy at a family picnic in the middle of the summer and I still ate like a teenage boy at a family picnic in the middle of the summer. I always felt like Mama thought that I should have let my wealth affect me more than it did. It wasn't that she didn't like who I was. I was her only son. She just wanted me to separate myself from the darkness that chased both of us. It was almost as though she thought that as soon as my software career took off or when I finally sold the program that brought me enough to disappear into the woods, I should be eating nothing but lobster and caviar and washing it all down with swigs of champagne. I had never been able to develop a taste for that stuff. I stuck to my sandwiches, potato salad, and beer.

The pain in my leg was getting worse, but I continued to stand, knowing that if I sat down, even for a few minutes, the pain would be much worse when I stood again. It was better to just push through until the end of the day. As I leaned against the counter eating, occasionally tossing a chip or piece of meat down to Scout, I peered out of the picture window and wondered about the smoke coming from the cabin down the mountain. I wondered what kind of people had decided to rent the cabin. Was it a family? A couple on their honeymoon, wanting some privacy and dreaming of the romance of snowflakes drifting gently around them? I sincerely hoped that wasn't the case. Unless they were very familiar with the mountain and the dangers that it could present, they weren't going to think that the snow was so romantic after the first couple of feet fell.

When I finished my lunch, I rinsed the plate and tucked it into the dishwasher. Sometimes I felt guilty for even having a dishwasher. Scout didn't use many dishes, which meant that I often ran the appliance when there were only a couple of plates, bowls, and utensils inside. It wasn't the most efficient use of energy, but no matter how long I spent on the mountain, washing dishes by hand was just something I couldn't stand. There were still a few hours left of daylight and I had work to finish. I turned to call Scout to come out with me, but I found him curled up in front of the wood-burning stove, sound asleep. He was all the family I needed now. I smiled at the little deserter and walked back outside into air that was already feeling distinctly colder.

Chapter Three

Charlotte

I wish I could have slept later the next morning, but just as I always did, I was up when the sun had barely lightened the horizon. I laid in the narrow wooden bed and stared at the ceiling for several minutes before I moved. I didn't want to climb out from the warm cocoon created by the quilt. The frost creating a beautiful sparkling pattern across the window panes told me that the temperature had dropped overnight. I dreaded emerging into the chill of the cabin, but even more, I dreaded facing my family. Even though they had spent the rest of the evening acting as though the argument had never happened, I knew that I needed to make my apologies. I had overreacted to the situation and I knew that my sisters didn't deserve to have their joy dampened by my sensitivity. Finally, I braced myself and swung my legs over the side of the bed. My toes touched the wooden floor and I felt them recoil. The planks were like ice and sent a sharp, stinging shiver through my body. I held my feet up for a few seconds, then took a deep breath and jumped out of the bed. I immediately scurried over to my slippers and bathrobe and wrapped myself tightly in them. I knew that the rest of the family was still sleeping. Unlike me, their bodies weren't unshakably tied to their sleep routine. If they didn't have a specific reason for getting up early, they didn't. I knew that the little ones would be waking up soon enough and that would mean the domino effect of wakening for the rest of the adults, so I cherished the few moments of solitude that I had.

Grasping my toiletry bag and clothes for the day to my chest, I scurried out of the room and rushed to the nearby bathroom. A long shower thawed me out and by the time that I had dried and styled my hair, dressed, and done my makeup, I felt as prepared as I could for the day. I went to the kitchen and explored the cabinets until I found a coffee maker and supplies. Soon the smell of fresh, dark coffee filled the cabin. Filling a cup, I walked out of the back door onto an enclosed porch. It was colder out here than it was inside the cabin, but the walls did provide some protection from the chill outside. I stood close to one of the floor-to-ceiling windows and stared out over the peaceful morning. The sun had just risen, and rays of golden light were glowing in the rich hues of red, yellow, and orange of the foliage. These colors stood in bold contrast to the green of the towering pines. I took a long sip of the coffee and let out a sigh as the hot liquid seeped through my body. I heard footsteps behind me and I turned to see Madeline step out onto the porch with me. She, too, was holding a steaming mug in one hand, but the little paper label hanging over one side told me that she had opted for herbal tea rather than the coffee.

She smiled at me as she stepped up beside me and looked out over the woods as I had been doing. She took a sip of her tea and sighed. I smiled. Even though there were so many things about us that were so different, it was nice when I noticed the ways that all us sisters were alike.

"Listen, Madeline, I wanted to tell you how sorry I am for the way that I acted last night."

"Oh, Charlotte," she said, turning to me and shaking her head so that her thick ringlets bounced around her shoulders. "You don't have to say that you're sorry."

"Yes, I do," I said. "I shouldn't have reacted like that. That was your moment and I was horrible about it."

Madeline looked back at the window and gave a little shrug.

"You did kind of steal my thunder," she said.

I made a big gasp of mock horror and gently nudged my sister. She laughed and then shot me a playful glare.

"Hey, be careful. I'm pregnant, you know."

"I know," I said. "And I'm so happy for you. I know that this is what you and William have wanted since you got married."

"We have," she said, suddenly looking dreamy and whimsical, almost like she was looking through me into some vision of her future. "I still can't believe it's true." She pressed her hands to her belly and looked down at them. "I've never been happier."

I wished that I knew what to say to her. I was happy for her. I truly was. But I couldn't connect with the sheer joy that was on her face. Madeline looked up at me and I saw her expression change. She looked slightly drawn, as if she was worried about me.

"I guess that you and Miranda will have a lot to talk about this week," I said, hoping to distract her and push past the look she was giving me.

"We will," she agreed. "But I'd like to talk to you, too."

"What do you want to talk to me about?" I asked casually, taking a sip from my coffee.

"Charlotte, you know that they don't mean any harm. They only want what's best for you."

"That's what they say," I said.

"You don't believe them?"

"It's hard to believe that someone wants the best for you when all they do is criticize you and imply that you've somehow ruined their lives by not getting married and having children."

"I don't think that they think that you've ruined their lives," Madeline said. "But you have to admit, it is strange."

"What's strange?"

"How much you've changed."

I looked at my sister, surprised by the comment. There were many things that I expected her to say, but that wasn't one of them.

"I've changed?" I asked incredulously. "That's what this is all supposed to be about? How have I changed?"

"Well," she said, her voice quieter now as if she were trying to keep me calm. "We all thought that you would be the first one to get married. You and Daniel have been together forever."

"Had," I emphasized. "Had been together forever. We aren't together anymore."

"You had been together forever," Madeline corrected herself. "You two had been together for years even before Miranda met Seth. All of us thought that the two of you were just going to run off into the sunset and have this absolutely amazing life together. There were pools to see when you were going to drop out of college so that you could go ahead and get married." She took a breath. "But you never did."

"Nope," I said my emotions suddenly feeling dulled as I looked at her, feeling as though she were just another of the people looking down on me. No longer my little sister, she was part of the wall that I felt had formed between me and some semblance of a life. "We never did. And you know what? You're right. I have changed. I've changed so much. But all for the better. I'm stronger now. More confident. I feel like I've finally found myself. And while it might be hard for you and the others to believe, and it's difficult to really experience sometimes, I'm happier, too."

"How could you be happier?" Madeline asked. "It's only been a few months since the two of you broke up, and you won't even talk about what happened. You've spent so much of your life with him, Charlotte. How can you be happier now that he's not here?"

Because it was feeling strong and confident that gave me what I needed to actually leave him.

I opened my mouth to say it, but I couldn't. I didn't know how much of my history with Daniel, Madeline knew. With as dismissive as my mother was when I told her that I was unhappy and even afraid of Daniel, even going so far as to tell me that I was being too dramatic being so upset the night that he slapped me hard enough to bring the taste of blood to my lips and a faint bruise to my cheekbone that made my application of makeup thick for several days. That night I ran home to my mother, wanting her comfort, wanting to tell her what happened, only to learn that Daniel had already called her. He wanted to make sure that I was alright, Violet told me. He said that I was in a fit and stumbled on the steps and he tried to catch me. She believed him. I went back to my apartment, waiting for him to show up, and cried.

Madeline had seemed so young when that happened. Far too young for me to confide in her about what I was going through. I would never blame anyone but Daniel for what I had gone through with him. The only thing I could blame myself for was how long I stayed. There were times, though, when I wondered how my parents could have missed it. How they could have seen how a relationship that had begun when we were young teenagers had gone so quickly from doting to jealous to controlling to abusive. That word still felt bitter and out of place on my tongue. Though I had finally come to a time when I was able to accept that that was what it was, what it had always been, I felt strange putting voice to it, or even thinking it. Confidence had come to me slowly and gradually, but once I found it, my self-awareness had come quickly, explosively, and the relationship had crumbled. There were days when I felt like I was still pulling myself out of the rubble. But I was there. I was surviving.

My little sister wasn't so young now. She gazed at me through the eyes of a wife and soon to be a mother. I hoped that those eyes would be different than the ones that had looked at me. I hoped that they would see if her child needed her. For now, they were eyes that stared at me as though they were searching for the person I used to be. I wanted to tell her why my relationship with Daniel had ended, but I didn't know if she would believe me. I didn't know if she would be capable of accepting it as reality. I had seen that so much. People wanted to believe in love. They wanted to believe that the beautiful, well-bred couples who had been together their whole lives would continue on for the rest of them. They didn't want to think that there was so much more to the relationship when doors closed, and smiles faded.

I knew that it wouldn't do any good to tell Madeline what had happened between us. Not yet, anyway. Maybe someday there would be a time when I would tell each of my sisters. For now, I just wanted to put it behind me. I wanted to let the holiday happen and then go home and continue to move forward. I knew that the harder I pushed back against any of them, the more unpleasant it was going to become, and that wasn't what I wanted from this week.

"Right now, I'm happier because I'm here with my family," I told her.

Before she could say anything else, we heard the sound of four little feet running down the steps followed by the slower, less enthusiastic steps of the other adults in the house. The sun was fully risen now. The morning had really begun.

We spent the rest of the day together, playing games, sharing memories, and going through the packets of food that the cook had sent along with my parents, along with detailed instructions on how to prepare the Thanksgiving meal. They couldn't understand why I found this so hilarious, and for the first time in as long as I could remember, I started to feel like the family was really coming together and I was able to relax. I was lying across the bed in my room reading in the late afternoon, enjoying the peaceful quiet that had fallen over the cabin when both of Miranda's children had gone down for a nap when I heard my mother's voice from the front of the house.

"You're here!" she exclaimed happily.

I thought that one of the children might have woken up and snuck downstairs to try to surprise her, but then I heard her calling for me. I reluctantly put down my book and slipped my feet back into my slippers so that I could shuffle out into the rest of the house. I was coming around the corner, starting to ask when we would eat dinner, when my blood ran cold and my steps halted beneath me. I felt my hands trembling and a tightness in my throat that made it hard to breathe.

"Hello, Charlie."

My name isn't Charlie. My name is Charlotte.

I couldn't bring the words to my lips. I felt like my voice had died in my throat and there was nothing that I could do to force it forward.

"Charlotte?" My mother said, a hint of urging in her voice like she was trying to cajole a child into saying thank you for a gift from a distant relative. "Don't you have something to say?"

"What are you doing here?"

The perfect, cultured smile on Daniel's face didn't change as he took a step toward me.

"I came to see you, Charlie."

"Isn't it sweet?" my mother asked, fairly gushing as she stepped up beside Daniel and put a hand on either shoulder, giving him a squeeze as she guided him forward another step.

"What are you doing here?" I asked again. "Why are you here?"

"Well, Charlotte, what a silly question," my mother said.

"Daniel got in touch with us," my father said, stepping into the entryway from the living room. "We've been talking over the last several weeks."

I turned to look at my father, not believing that I had really heard what I thought that I had just heard.

"You've what?" I asked.

"Daniel called us," my father continued. "He has been so worried about you and he wanted to make sure that you were doing alright."

"Worried about me?"

I felt like I had been reduced to just repeating what people were saying around me, not able to fully form a thought of my own.

"Yes," my mother said. "He's just been sick with worry."

Did people actually say that?

Daniel took another step toward me and I fought not to take a step back from him. I didn't want him to see me back down from him or to show the fear that was creeping up the back of my neck.

"Why?" I asked.

"Why?" Daniel asked, manufactured concern making his voice high. "Charlie, you don't need to lie. You don't need to pretend. You're safe. We're your family. It's alright to talk about what's been bothering you."

"What do you mean?"

"Don't worry, honey. It's OK," my father said. "Daniel told us that you've been going through a lot of stress with work and that you might have gotten into some situations that you haven't known how to handle. That's what caused you to end your relationship so hastily."

"But it's alright," Daniel said, taking another step closer and reaching for my hand. "I understand. I know that things can get difficult when you are trying to have it all, but you don't have to impress anyone."

That was the moment I noticed that there were snowflakes on his shoulders and melting in his hair. It had begun to snow outside, but what I would have usually found magical was lost on me in that moment.

"Daniel reassured us that he has no hard feelings," my mother said. "He's not angry with you. He loves you and wants you to know that he's here for you."

"Violet and Greg were gracious enough to invite me to come up here and spend Thanksgiving with the family. It will give us time to reconnect."

Violet and Greg.

I knew that Daniel had known my parents for most of his life, even before the two of us started dating in high school, but the familiarity with which he talked about them made my skin crawl. I looked at my parents, both of whom were gazing at me with hope in their eyes, and then at my sisters, who stood just inside the living room, watching cautiously.

"You invited him here?" I asked.

I managed to keep my voice steady, but I could feel the trembling in my throat and the pain in my jaw as I struggled to maintain it.

"We thought that it would be a nice surprise," Violet said. "You've been so tense recently and after your explosion last night...I thought that seeing Daniel again and hearing that he forgives you and still loves you would be just the thing that you need to have the most wonderful holiday season."

I felt like I had suddenly found myself in a movie. Nothing was real. Everyone around me was looking at me with wide eyes and urging smiles, but I could only feel horror filling my belly. I was so angry that I couldn't speak. I didn't know what I was supposed to say to any of them. In seconds the anger filled by belly until it ached, and I turned on my heel and rushed back into the bedroom that my mother had chosen for me as her opening salvo. I could hear Daniel reassure my parents and my sisters and then come after me, but I ignored him. I burst into the bedroom, grabbed my suitcase out from under the bed and began to shove clothes into it. I walked down the hall to the bathroom, grabbed my toiletries, and stalked back into my room, finding Daniel already standing there. I walked around him to the bed and forced the toiletry bag inside. Finally, I whipped around to face him.

"What do you think you're doing here?"

"Exactly what I said," Daniel said, the sweet, innocent smile that he had been wearing in the entryway gone now. "I'm here to see you, Charlie."

"Stop calling me that," I demanded. "I told you that I hate that."

"Why? It's what I've always called you."

"And I've always hated it."

As a final thought I grabbed the book that I had been reading when my mother called me and forced it into the corner of the suitcase, slamming the top down and pulling the zipper around.

"I can't believe that you have the balls to come here."

I was terrified, extremely aware that we were alone in the small room. But I wanted him to see my anger. I wanted him to see that I was stronger now and that he didn't have the same effect on me that he used to.

"I was invited."

"I don't know what you said to them, but I don't want you here."

I started to walk towards the door, but Daniel reached out and took my elbow, pulling me back into the room. Just that touch was enough twist my stomach and make my throat tighten.

"Don't be that way, Charlie," he said. "Aren't you at all happy to see me?"

"No."

"Please, Charlie. Just give me a chance. I've told you how sorry I am."

His voice had changed. Gone was the hint of arrogance that have been there when I first came into the bedroom, replaced now by the slick tone that I had learned to recognize as being purely manipulative. This is how he had drawn me back in so many times before. He had stared at me with the eyes that he knew I had fallen in love with when I was just a young teenager. He would tell me that he was sorry, admit that everything that he had done had been so wrong and that I didn't deserve any of it. He would beg for my forgiveness, promising me that everything is going to be different and that we were going to be so happy together. Sweeping, dramatic claims of love and devotion, extreme statements of not being able to survive without me were enough to pull me away from the anger, hurt, and sadness that I was feeling and draw me back to him. It happened countless times before. Too many times for me to remember each individually. They blended together until all I remembered was the sound of his voice and the cloying, repetitive words.

"Get away from me," I said.

I pushed past Daniel and stomped through the house toward the front door. My father tried to step in front of me, but I pulled my suitcase in front of me, creating a blockage that seemed to push him back.

"Where are you going?" my mother nearly shrieked from the living room as I pushed through the door and out into the beginning of the sunset.

"Madeline, I'm borrowing your car," I called by way of a response.

I knew Madeline well enough to know that she and William would have come in two separate cars. Several years older than her, William was already a highly sought-after surgeon and would often receive urgent calls requiring him to rush back to the hospital. After this had resulted in her sitting in the waiting room for several hours or calling one of us to come get her, Madeline learned to travel separately from her husband so that if he did get a call summoning him to the hospital, she could stay wherever they were and still be able to go wherever she needed to. I also knew her well enough to know that, despite warnings and urgings from all of us, Madeline always left her keys in her ignition.

I tossed my suitcase into the backseat and climbed behind the wheel, slamming the door closed just as Daniel rushed up to the side of the car. Squinting into the snow that was falling steadily, I slammed on the gas and sped away from the cabin. I quickly realized that I didn't know where I was going. I had been too busy staring at the passing trees and feeling the texture of the road change beneath me to pay attention to the twists and turns that we had taken as we arrived, and the snow was falling harder and faster with each passing moment, making it almost impossible to see in front of me. I found myself on a road that seemed to be spiraling upwards along the mountain and I knew that that wasn't what I wanted to be doing. I needed to get to the bottom of the mountain where I could make my way home. I promised myself that I would never again allow anyone to pick me up from my house to bring me anywhere. I was going to follow in Madeline's lead and always have my own car with me.

The snow outside seemed to have followed my mood, turning from a gradual fall to a raging storm in moments, and the windshield ahead of me was nearly solid white. I slowed the car until it was creeping along the road, pressing forward as far as I could until I could see the slight change in color along the side of the road that I was following that told me there was another access road. Confident that this was the road that would lead me down the mountain, I turned onto it and headed down.

I knew that I shouldn't. I knew that the snow and ice were covering the road and making every narrow inch more treacherous. But the anger that was flowing through me was enough to take away all reason and I pressed steadily on the gas, increasing my speed and pushing me faster until I felt the car leave my control and become at the mercy of the slick surface of the road. I hadn't been listening to the radio that afternoon at the cabin or the evening when I climbed into Madeline's car and sped away. If I had, I might have heard the warnings about the storm. If I had, I might have heard that the storm had already taken down a tree that was now laying across the road ahead of me.

My foot pressed hard against the brake pedal, trying desperately to get the car back under my control. I fought to hold the wheel straight so that it didn't turn wildly and so that I had some chance of moving down the road in a direct path rather than weaving. Ahead of me the snow was falling in a thick blanket, the individual flakes almost imperceptible in the sky. Suddenly I could see something dark looming across the road. It completely blocked my way and there was nothing that I could do. In the brief instant that I had, I considered my options, then took a breath and turned the wheel as hard as I could. The back of the car swung around, smashing into the tree. The jolt caused my head to snap forward into the steering wheel and I felt a sharp pain go through my forehead, then everything went still.

Chapter Four

Micah

The radio set up in my living room was pouring out a never-ending stream of warnings. What had been the occasional reminder that severe weather might be on its way had become forceful demands for attention, telling the few of us that were on the mountain to be prepared for the worst, and telling those who might have interest in coming up to stay away. There hadn't been weather this severe this early in the season in years, and though I had dedicated myself to being as prepared as possible and knew that I was going to be able to weather the storm just fine, I found myself wondering about the people in the cabin below me. The smoke from the chimney had continued since I first noticed it, telling me that they were keeping a fire burning at all times. It was likely their idea of creating holiday ambiance, not realizing how important their fireplace and stove would be as the temperatures continued to drop and the electricity was at risk of going out. I hoped that they were either better prepared than I thought that they would be, or that they were already putting in calls to the rangers who would put plans into place to rescue them if necessary.

I had been hearing the warnings about a tree that had come down across the access road and my curiosity was getting the better of me. From the description of the place where it had fallen, it seemed that it wasn't too far from my lodge. Considering that I was the only one who lived this far up on the mountain, that meant that it shouldn't cause problems for anyone lower down. While this was a benefit to them, it also meant that the motivation to get the tree off of the road wasn't very high and it would likely remain low on the priority list throughout the storm. That didn't really matter much to me. I had everything that I needed and would have no need to head down the mountain anytime soon. Having a day without going out into the woods to work, however, was starting to create cabin fever and I needed to get out for a little while. Going to see the tree seemed like the ideal excuse. I strapped on my snowshoes, lured Scout away from the wood stove with the promise of playing, and headed out.

The snow was more intense than I had expected it to be, but my stubbornness wouldn't allow me to turn back around. Being in the thickest part of the woods provided some protection from the snow and I was able to move more quickly without the flakes stinging on my skin. Scout romped around me happily, occasionally dropping into a deeper drift and sinking until he was almost out of sight, then bounding out again. I tossed a stick ahead of me and watched as he ran toward it, sniffed it, then promptly lost interest. We were nearly to the access road when I heard the sound of gears grinding and a sickening crunch. I knew that sound. It was all too familiar to me. The pain in my leg pulsed as if in acknowledgment, and I shook it hard, trying to force away the sensation and the thoughts that it brought with it.

Calling Scout to me, I increased my pace, pushing through the snow toward the road and the sound of the crash. I dreaded what I was going to see when I came over the ridge and looked down at the tree. The sound had been deep and crushing, enough to tell me that it was serious and the damage could be severe. I stepped up onto the top of the ridge and looked down. The snow blowing in the wind was still too much for me to be able to see clearly, but I could make out the hint of the road weaving through. I hurried down toward the road, my snowshoes preventing me from maintaining as fast of a pace as I would have wanted to, and soon saw the road ahead of me. The narrow passage was bordered on one side by the sharp rocks of the mountain and on the other by a sheer drop. The sound of the crunching had made my stomach drop, making me think that the car might have tumbled over the edge. As I approached the road, however, I saw that that wasn't the case.

The massive tree blocked the entire road, the width of its trunk so expansive that it rose up from the ground over the top of the car. I noticed that it wasn't the front of the car that had smashed into the tree, but rather the back, crushing the little white sedan's trunk into its backseat, but leaving the front fairly unscathed except for a small impact from swinging around after hitting. The angle was strange, and I wondered if the driver had positioned the car that way intentionally. If they had, it was a smart move. Though the car was now a permanent Christmas ornament on the massive tree, turning around prevented the front end from flattening. As it was, the driver's side of the car seemed to have gotten through whatever had brought the car to rest in this position without damage. I walked toward it, wondering who could be driving and why they were up this high on the mountain, using a road that only I ever used. As I got close to the car, however, and was able to see into the driver's side window, the relief I had felt disappeared.

Because of the angle of the car and the fact that it was the back that had crashed into the tree, I had assumed that whoever had been driving had either gotten out and tried to continue on foot, or would be sitting in the front seat already on their phone trying to find a rescuer. Instead, I saw that there was someone behind the wheel and they were draped over the steering wheel, limp and silent. I grasped the handle of the driver's side door and pulled. It wouldn't budge. It was a new model car, something that had likely been driven off the lot within the last few months, which meant that the locks had engaged automatically when the driver started moving. I brushed the snow off of the window and leaned close to the glass, resting my face against my cupped hands to get a better view of the inside of the car. I could see the driver better now and recognized that it was a woman. She was resting on the steering wheel, her head leaned against the top and her hands wrapped around each side. The tightness of the grip around the wheel told me that despite her appearance, she wasn't unconscious. I knocked lightly on the window, not wanting to scare her, but needing her to unlock the door so that I could check on her.

The woman inside jumped when she heard me knock and turned to look at me.

"Unlock the door!" I shouted through the window.

The wind around me had picked up and was starting to wail. She shook her head and I knocked on the window again.

"Unlock the door!" I repeated. "You need to get out of the car."

She looked around as if she had forgotten that she was in the car at all and had no idea what had happened. Seeming to recognize the severity of the situation, she sat up slowly and reached for the lock button. I heard it click and pulled the handle again. As soon as I opened the door, Scout rushed forward, wriggling around me to look into the car at the woman. She didn't recoil from him, even when he hopped up so that his cold, wet paws landed in her lap. I had intended on making him wear boots, but every time that I had tried, he freaked out, shaking his feet and trying his hardest not to keep any of his paws on the ground. He had jumped up and landed with his face in the snow so many times that I eventually gave up and just added drying his paws when we got inside out of routine.

The woman reached down and stroked his head, leaning down slightly to look at him.

"Are you alright?" I asked.

The woman lifted her head and looked at me. My eyes met hers and I felt a flicker of something in the back of my mind. It felt like recognition, but I couldn't quite bring myself to know what it was about her that was familiar, or who she might be. I asked her again and she gave a slow nod. It was as though all of her movements were stretched out, like she was moving through water.

"I think so," she said.

"Come on," I said, patting Scout's side to get him away from her and then reaching into the car for her. "We need to get you out of the car."

She wasn't wearing a seatbelt, making it easy for me to scoop her up and help her climb out. When she turned to face me fully I noticed a cut on her forehead. It wasn't serious, just enough to create a small trickle of blood, and it seemed to be her only injury. She was fully on her feet, but suddenly her legs seemed to give out beneath her and she slumped against me. I grabbed onto her, holding her tightly against me with one arm while I reached around to close the door with the other. The woman didn't seem to be capable of walking through the growing storm on her own, so I scooped her into my arms and carried her up the ridge and into the woods. Under the protection of the trees I was less concerned about her, but the soft moans coming from her made me wonder if her injury was more serious than I had originally thought. I knew that she needed to get out of the cold and snow, and it would be a while before any type of rescue would be able to get to her. The only choice I had was to bring her to the lodge and keep her warm and safe.

I carried the woman into the house and brought her to the back hallway and into the guest room. This was one of the features of the lodge that I had included when designing it because the builder insisted that guest rooms were just something that homes had, but had never actually been used. Now I was glad that I had it as I stretched the woman out across the comforter and looked down at her. Her face was peaceful and comfortable now, and her breath was even. It no longer looked like she had passed out, but rather that she was asleep. Scout tromped into the room after me and looked up at the bed as if questioning me about the woman. I looked down at him.

"She's going to need us to take care of her for a while," I told Scout. "I'm going to go back to her car and see if I can find anything that she might need. You stay here and watch over her."

As if he fully understood what I had told him, Scout jumped up on the end of the bed and curled into a ball close to the woman's feet. He rested his head on his paws as if to fall asleep, but kept his eyes open, staring at her. I hurried back through the lodge and stepped out on the porch, taking a moment to stamp the snow off of my feet and shake it off of my arms. I knew that more would take its place in a matter of minutes, but I figured I shouldn't give it a head start. I made my way back through the woods, my progress slower this time because of the dusk that had settled through the woods. The combination of the darkness of the evening and the snow that was still swirling through the air made it harder for me to get through the trees and I reached into the pocket of my heavy coat to pull out the flashlight that I always kept there. The beam did little to slice through the thick blackness of the woods, but I shined it on the snow ahead of me so that at least I could see if there were any obstacles that would cause me to trip. I was relieved when I made it to the edge of the ridge and could carefully ease my way back down onto the road.

I opened the car and was thankful for the overhead dome light that popped on. I looked around the cabin of the car, trying to find any personal belongings that the woman might have had with her. That strange tickle of recognition was still in the back of my mind and I dug through my memories, trying to figure out why I felt like I knew her, what was familiar about her. I hadn't had much opportunity to look at her, but somehow the curve of her face seemed to me like I had seen it before. A sudden thought came to my mind. It was more like a flash than a true memory. I seemed to remember the woman, her face younger and softer, in the halls of my high school many years before. That girl had been quiet and shy, seeming to exist just on the edge of the popular crowd that I all but ruled. My place in the crowd had been earned by my position on the football team, secured even before freshman year had begun. Hers was different. That girl, whose name I couldn't seem to bring to my tongue, was able to move through the most popular group in the school thanks to the wealth of her family. I wondered if it could be possible that this woman could be the same girl who I was remembering. And if it was, how did she end up on the mountain, so close to my lodge?

Out of the corner of my eye I noticed what looked like the corner of a suitcase. It seems to have once been placed on the back seat of the car, but the impact of the back of the car into the tree had sent it on to the floorboards and wedged it in between the front seats. I grasped the handle and pulled. It gave only a couple of inches and then remained in place. I grabbed onto it with my other hand and I moved it back and forth, maneuvering it until it finally came loose. The suitcase seemed somewhat crumpled, but other than that was intact. I put it on the passenger seat and leaned down to look between the front seat at the floorboards and what of the backseat I could still see. It didn't look like there was anything else in the car. The idea that she had traveled with only one small suitcase struck me as odd, but I still didn't know where she could have come from or how long she had intended to spend on the mountain. I thought about looking in the glove compartment to see if there might be a license or something else that could identify her, but I changed my mind. Bringing her a suitcase that was in plain sight was one thing, but digging through her glove compartment was another. I pulled the keys out of the ignition, locked the doors, and grabbed the suitcase. Ducking my head down against the wind and the snowflakes, I made my way back to the lodge.

I brought the suitcase into the guest room and checked on the woman. She was still lying on the bed, but head turned slightly so she lay partially on her side, still sleeping quietly. Scout lifted his head and looked at me as if to tell me that he had been watching over her and that she was still fine. I patted his head and told him he was a good boy. Apparently, this was enough to relieve him of his duties and he jumped down off the bed and headed into the kitchen to eat. I carefully untied the woman's boots and pulled them off of her feet and draped a blanket over her. I looked at the cut on her forehead again. I noticed that while the blood seemed to be drying, the cut was significant enough that I wanted to make sure it was covered. I went into the bathroom and came back with a damp cloth and a bandage. Moving as carefully as I could so as not to disturb her, I gently cleaned the cut. The fact that she had fallen forward and rested her head on the steering wheel seemed to have spread the blood, making the cut seem more serious than it really was, and I was relieved to see that it was smaller than I had originally thought. The woman groaned slightly in her sleep and I paused to look down at her. She was beautiful even though streaks of makeup down her cheeks were testament that she had gone through something before the car crashed into the tree.

As I went back to cleaning her forehead and putting a bandage over it, my mind continued to search through memories to find her. I saw her again, standing in the hallway, looking at me around the arm of a girl standing much closer. The girl standing closer to me was Staci Boyer, a cheerleader who was eyeing me to finish her football team bed-hopping bingo board. She was bold and forward, willing to do and say anything that she thought that I wanted her to just to get my attention. That had been thrilling when I was younger and first discovering my place in the popular crowd of the high school, but now it was boring at best, disturbing at worst. What was catching my attention at that moment was the shy, quiet girl.

Charlotte.

Her name came to me suddenly, rushing back into my mind as I remembered her noticing that I was looking at her. Her cheeks had reddened, and she had turned away suddenly, scurrying away down the hallway. There had been something about her then that had piqued my interest, making me wonder about her, and I was still wondering about her now as I watched her sleep for a few moments. Why was she on my mountain? What had brought her up this far to a place that I had chosen specifically because of its distance from people? I didn't know what might have brought her to the narrow, dangerous road that led down the mountain, and the thoughts and feelings that were coursing through me were strange and tangled, I couldn't determine if I was glad that she was there, glad to see her again, or if she was an intrusion in the solitude that I had carefully crafted for myself in the lodge.

Scout appeared back at the door to the bedroom and then walked to the bed, hopping up and resuming his position curled up at Charlotte's feet. He looked up at me as if to tell me that my services were no longer needed, and I smiled.

"Alright, boy. You go ahead and watch over her. Make sure she's OK. I'm going to go try to relax a little."

Scout watched me walk out of the room and when I glanced back in after looking away he had his head rested on his feet again. Confident that Charlotte was safe and comfortable for the time being, I walked out of the guest room and through the lodge to the room in the back hall, a room that I often kept locked even though no one else came into the house. Locking it somehow seemed to keep what was inside more secure, as though it couldn't affect me as much when it was locked away. That way I could go into it when I wanted to, when I needed to, and avoid it when I didn't.

Chapter Five

Charlotte

I didn't immediately open my eyes when I woke up. I laid there for a few seconds, feeling strange and disoriented. I couldn't remember falling asleep or what had happened in the minutes before I laid down. I felt the soft pillow beneath my head and the blanket draped over me, and realized that I didn't know where I was or how I had gotten there. I slowly lifted my eyelids, not knowing what I was going to see when my eyes opened fully, and found myself staring at a window. The curtains were pulled back and the space beyond the glass was impenetrably dark. I couldn't see anything beyond the blurry reflection that was created by the light filtering from an open door behind me. I sat up, looking around, trying to orient myself in the space, but there was nothing around me that was even slightly familiar. I didn't know where I was or what had gotten me there. I looked back at the reflection in the window and a sinking feeling came to my belly as unfamiliar eyes stared back at me.

I didn't know who I was.

It was a feeling that I couldn't explain, one that both fell over me heavily and seemed to creep down my body, making me shiver. I felt like I was a visitor within my body, not knowing anything about myself or what was happening to me. I didn't even know how long I had been sleeping or what had happened that caused me to sleep so deeply. As I sat up I noticed an ache in my head and I pressed my hand to it. My shifting on the bed seemed to have disrupted the dog laying at the foot of the bed and he lifted his head to look at me with soulful eyes. I wished that I recognized him. I wished that I knew his name or where he came from. Was he my dog? Had he been a part of my life for a long time? Being curled so close to me as I slept gave me comfort even if I didn't really know anything about him, and I leaned over to stroke his head. He nuzzled me, turning his head so that it rested in my palm.

"I guess I can't just stay here in bed forever," I said to him. "Maybe I'll remember where I am if I look around."

I started to climb out of the bed and noticed the side table. A cup of water sat beside a bottle of pain relievers. I poured a few of the pills out into my palm and popped them into my mouth, chasing them down with a gulp of water. The moment that the water hit my throat I realized how thirsty I was and swallowed down the rest of the cup before getting out of the bed. I had taken a few steps toward the door when I noticed a mirror hanging on the wall. I glanced into it, seeing the same unfamiliar reflection as I had seen in the window pane. This one was clearer, however, and I was able to see a bandage secured across my forehead, explaining the pain that I was feeling. I wondered what had happened and reached up to gingerly pull away the bandage. The cut beneath it was small, giving me a sense of relief, and I covered it back up.

Heading toward the light that was coming into the bedroom through the open door, I started to explore my surroundings. I looked around with every step, waiting for something to trigger my memories, to jog something in my mind that would shake me out of the fog that had fallen over me. The further that I moved away from the bedroom, however, the more disoriented and lost I felt. Nothing looked or felt familiar. The light was coming to me from a large open great room and I stepped into it with a sense of awe. It was gorgeous and expansive, an impressive balance between rustic and exquisite. I walked through it slowly, letting my fingertips run along the back of the couch. The brown leather was like butter beneath my skin and a dark grey and black crocheted blanket draped across one end gave the impression of a casual scene.

The building around me seemed still and quiet, as though there was no one else there with me. I didn't know if I should find that reassuring or disconcerting. Was there supposed to be someone else here with me? If so, who was it? A sudden thought brought my hand to my pocket. My phone was there, and I picked it up. The screen told me that I had no reception and I tucked it away. Just as the phone left my fingertips, a wailing sound from outside startled me. I took a few steps toward a window and peered out. There was a light just outside the window, allowing me to see the fiercely swirling snow. There was another wail and I realized that it was the wind screaming through the trees as it picked up the drifts and sliced through the air. It was obvious that the storm was quite severe, meaning that it would be impossible for me to leave that night.

I moved through the great room and into a smaller den-like room. The great room had featured a tremendous fireplace that took up the majority of one wall, but this room had a large black wood burning stove. There was a fire burning in its belly, sending its comforting warmth out into the room. I was tempted to curl up in one of the large arm chairs positioned on either side of a knotted rug, but the hollow emptiness in my belly kept me moving through the house. I wondered how long it had been since I had eaten. The hunger making my stomach growl made it seem as though it had been quite some time. I continued to explore the sprawling house, eventually finding my way to the kitchen. It was an incredibly strange sensation to wonder where I was and if I belonged here. I didn't know if I was a stranger in this place as I was in my own body, or if this was my home and I simply couldn't remember. I wanted to believe that if I was somewhere that mattered to me, that held precious memories, that I would remember. I wanted to think that I would be able to feel the energy of myself or people who I cared about in the space. Yet at the same time I didn't know who I was or who I cared about, so how would I even know that those memories were there?

I was confusing myself and I tried to push the thoughts out of my mind as I crossed the wide stone floor to the massive refrigerator. I opened it and began to pull things out and spread them across the counter. Then I went to a door that I assumed was a pantry. I opened it and found it to be nothing more than a small closet that contained a coat, a jacket, a pair of boots, and a large trash can. I closed the door and moved across the room to another door. This one did reveal the pantry and I pulled out a few more containers. My hunger seemed to have gotten the best of me as I went to work preparing the different foods that I had taken out. I heard a faint clicking sound and looked toward the entrance to the kitchen to see the black and white dog that had been curled on the bed with me, walking into the kitchen. It was reassuring to see him there with me, almost as though he were guarding me as I tried to navigate where I was and what was happening. I leaned down to pet him, scratching at his neck. My fingers hit a collar and I ran them around its edge to find the tags hanging at the front of his neck. I lifted them, but only found the engraved confirmation that he had received his vaccinations.

"His name is Scout."

The voice made me jump and I got to my feet quickly, but didn't step away from the dog. He was the only thing that had made me feel safe since I woke up and I didn't want to give up that comfort. I looked at the entrance to a hallway toward the back of the kitchen and saw a man standing there, staring at me. Though his expression was largely emotionless, he didn't look as though he were trying to frighten me, and I tried to keep myself calm.

"Scout?" I asked. I looked down at the dog again and then back at the man. "Really?"

"I know," he said as he stepped into the room. "It's not very creative. But it's the name that he had when I found him at the shelter and he never seemed to want to get used to anything else. He would only respond when I called him Scout, so that's what stuck."

"What other names did you try?" I asked.

"Sir Gawain. Viking. Amadeus."

I stared at him, trying to decide if he was being serious, and quickly realized that he was. I reached down and scratched Scout beneath his chin.

"I think that if I were him I would have only responded to Scout, too."

The man shrugged, stepping up to join me in petting Scout, who looked like he was nearly overcome with the sheer joy of the attention. The man was standing close to me now and I was able to look into his face. He was ruggedly handsome, a strong jaw and a thick beard and mustache making him look as though he was perfectly in place in the backdrop of the woods beyond the window. It was his eyes, though, that truly struck me. I found myself staring at them, feeling held in place by them. There was a flicker of something familiar, a spark in the back of my mind that told me that I had seen those eyes before. The feeling was fleeting though, and I wasn't able to grasp onto it enough to know what it was that I was remembering.

Did I know this man? Was it possible that we had some sort of relationship?

Could he be my husband?

The thought sent an unexpected thrill through me, but as soon as it did, I realized that the chances of that were slim. It was unlikely he would have told me the dog's name when he saw me looking at his tags if we were married. He also probably would have given me a warmer, more concerned greeting when he came into the room. Perhaps a kiss. The chill returned, and I felt my cheeks burn slightly.

Whether he noticed it or not, the man turned away from me and looked around the kitchen at the partially prepared snack that I had been working on when the dog came into the room.

"It looks like you have made yourself right at home," he said.

That was absolute confirmation that my assumption was correct. This wasn't my home. The burning on my cheeks increased and I heard myself stumbling over words, trying to find a way to explain myself.

"I'm sorry," was all that I could come up with.

"It's alright," he said.

"No, I'm sorry," I said, starting to feel a sense of panic forming in my stomach and rushing up my spine, making me feel like my breath was caught in my chest. "I don't remember anything. I don't know where I am or how I got here. I'm sorry."

I didn't know why I was feeling the way that I was and the feeling itself was as frightening as my emotions were apparently interpreting the situation to be. I felt like I needed to escape, to get out of the space and away from the man. There was a voice in the back of my mind, muffled shouting, words that I couldn't decipher but that made my heart clench. It was a memory, but not one that I had any more grasp on than anything else. I didn't know the voice, but it struck me that it didn't seem to be that of the man who was standing in front of me. He held up a hand as if to quiet me and Scout pushed closer to my legs.

"It's alright," he said again. "Calm down. I knew you were here. I'm the one who brought you here."

I took a breath, letting it fill my chest and then letting it out slowly to try to calm my shaking.

"You did?" I asked.

"Yes," he said, taking a cautious step toward me. "A few hours ago."

I shook my head, starting to feel even more confused than I had been.

"Why did you bring me here? What happened?"

"Don't be scared," he said. "You're not being held captive. I would say that you could leave at any time, but I think if you took a glance out the window you would see that that's not really the case."

"I saw," I said, nodding. "That's a pretty serious storm."

"It is," he agreed. "And incidentally, not only what is holding you here, not me, but what made it necessary for you to be here in the first place."

I knew that he was trying to be lighthearted and joke with me, but the more that he spoke, the more disoriented I felt.

"What?" I asked.

"How is your head feeling?" he asked.

"It hurts a little," I admitted.

"Come let me look at your forehead."

He gestured toward the small table that was nestled in a picture window at the front of the room. I sat down on one of the cushioned chairs and ran my fingers absently through Scout's fur as he rested his head on my lap. The man carefully peeled away the bandage and I felt him gently touching around the cut.

"It looks alright," he said. "It's not red or swollen, which is good."

"Are you a doctor?" I asked.

I realized with a touch of bemusement that I had asked that question sarcastically many times before, but this time I wasn't being nasty or trying to call someone out for acting as though they knew more than they did. This time, though, it was a completely genuine question.

Was that a memory, or just an impression of the type of person I am?

The man shook his head.

"Not a doctor," he said. "But when you live up here, you're pretty much in the wild. It's beneficial to pick up at least a cursory knowledge of first aid and potential injuries. I cleaned and dressed the cut to reduce the chances of infection. My only concern is a concussion. I've seen enough of them to be wary of the symptoms."

"You've seen a lot of concussions on the mountain?" I asked.

He looked at me and I saw his warm green eyes darken slightly, but he didn't respond.

"You said that you can't remember anything?" he asked, putting the bandage back in place.

I shook my head.

"No," I said. "Nothing. Was I drinking last night.... or earlier tonight?"

"Not that I know of," he said.

This startled me.

"You weren't with me?"

"No," he said. "I found your car crashed into a tree that fell during the storm. It's blocking the only access road heading down the mountain. You must not have been listening to the radio. There were warnings about it being there."

"I don't know if I heard them or not," I said. "I don't know I would have gone down that road if I had."

"You must have had your reasons," he said. "My name is Micah."

His introduction was abrupt, almost as though he realized that he hadn't given me his name and felt like we had gotten well beyond the point where we should at least know each other's names.

Unfortunately, I didn't know mine.

I stared at him, my mouth slightly open as if I was willing the name to come out spontaneously. After several seconds, I shook my head.

"I don't remember," I said. I felt ridiculous saying it. Your name isn't something that you remember. It's simply something that is a part of you. At least, it should be. "I don't know," I corrected myself.

Micah looked at me for a few long seconds and I felt heat creeping up the back of my neck and across my chest. I knew that his sultry eyes and the shape of his broad shoulders and muscled chest through his shirt weren't what I should be thinking about at that moment, but I couldn't tame the thoughts that were filling my mind. The flicker of familiarity was in his eyes again and I remembered that he said that I passed out after he found me. I wondered if I was remembering the brief moment I must have looked at him before going unconscious. Did I have my memory then? Was I myself in that moment?

"Charlotte," he said. "Do you think that your name might be Charlotte?"

I thought about it for a few seconds, letting the sound of the name tumble around in my thoughts. I was in an interesting position, one that I realized most people would never experience. I could literally create myself. I could determine who and what I was. Yet as I sat there looking at Micah, all I could think about was the touch of his hands on my skin and wanting to feel more. I told myself that this was a good thing. Somewhere deep inside me, a place where I couldn't yet touch, was the person I really was, and my mind was clinging to it, not allowing me to erase it completely. I thought about the name that he had said again.

Charlotte.

Something about the name felt comfortable, like it fit. Whether it was truly my name or not, it was something and I would go with it for now. I nodded.

"Alright," I said.

"Alright?" he asked.

"I don't know, but I like the way it sounds."

Chapter Six

Micah

Charlotte, if it was really her, hadn't reacted to my
name, but she hadn't reacted much to hers, either. I hadn't gotten
the confirmation about her identity that I had hoped for, but the
more time that I spent close to her, the more confident I was that
she was exactly who I thought. Looking into her eyes gave me the
same curious, undeniable pull that I had felt each time that I saw
her in the hallway or that one time when I glanced into the stands
during a game and saw her sitting, apart from the rest of the crowd,
watching. I never knew if she was actually watching me or if she was
just there, but seeing her sitting there had been unlike any other
time that I had looked into the crowd. I had been accustomed to the
praise then. The screaming of the girls and the shouts of the guys
fueled me, and I would look into the stands and pull out the
individual faces, making tallies of the people who had come to watch
me dominate the field. That night had been different. When I saw
her, everything else faded. The cheers became white noise and the
faces of everyone else in the stands became nothing but a blur. Only
she stood out.

It was brief, but that moment had stuck with me.
There was something so incredible about her, something that I
couldn't define, but also couldn't deny. That game I felt like I was
playing for her. But when I glanced back toward her at the end, she
wasn't there. Now I was looking at her again and for a second it felt

like I was looking back through the years and seeing her youthful, quiet face again. She was still young, but her face had changed. She was a woman now, the years having brought definition to her beauty and taking away some of the doubts from her eyes.

"Other than your head hurting, how are you feeling?"

"Fine, I guess."

"Are you dizzy?"

"No. Physically, I feel fine. I'm just confused. I don't feel like I'm injured enough to justify having no memory. I just wish I knew what happened."

"Sometimes even mild concussions can cause memory loss. I'm sure it's scary, but it's usually temporary."

"Usually?" she asked.

"There are never any guarantees."

About anything.

Part of me expected for her to dissolve, to panic, to be terrified, but she wasn't. Instead, Charlotte drew herself up with a deep breath and nodded as if to reassure herself as much as to reassure me. It looked like she was resigning herself to the fate of never regaining her memory, as though something in the past that she couldn't remember still had its hold on her, convincing her that if there were possibilities, it was most likely that she was going to experience the worst. I wondered what this must have meant for what she had gone through before ending up smashed against that tree, and in the years between the moment that I saw her in those stadium stands and when I found her.

"My phone doesn't have any service," she told me, reaching into her pocket and holding the phone out to me as if she felt she needed to prove what she was saying was true. She glanced down at it before putting it back in her pocket. "Even if it did, I wouldn't know who to call. "

"I'm sure that you have contacts listed in there," I said.

I meant it as a joke, hoping to take away some of the tension in her expression, but it seemed to have the opposite effect. She reached for her phone again and touched her finger to the back, opening the screen.

"I guess I could call..."

"No," I said, "it's alright. Most of the time there isn't much phone service up here if there's a storm."

"It's pretty serious out there, isn't it?" she asked.

"It is," I said, nodding. "The forecast best predicts that it's just going to keep going at least through tonight and likely tomorrow. It doesn't look like you're going to be able to go anywhere for a while."

"I'm sorry," she said. "I don't mean to impose on you."

"You're not imposing. I don't mind if you stay here for a while." I noticed an expression of uncertainty cross her eyes and I realize that the offer might be coming across as more intimidating than reassuring or hospitable. "There's another house on the property. It was the original home up here on the mountain and I stayed there while the lodge was being built. It's not too far from here. If you would rather, I can take you there and you can stay as long as you need to."

She looked at Scout and shook her head.

"No," she said. "If it's alright with you, I would rather stay here where the dog is."

I tried not to laugh. I didn't want her to feel as though I was making fun of her, but it seems to me that that was a funny way to make a decision about where to stay. Scout gave her hand a long, lazy lick and looked at her with those big eyes and I immediately changed my mind. If I had the option, I would probably want to stay where he was, too.

"Of course," I told her. "You're welcome to stay here with me, and Scout, until the storm blows over."

"Thank you," she said. "I don't feel like that's enough."

"What do you mean?"

"I don't feel like just saying thank you is enough. I don't know what I would have done if you hadn't found me."

I didn't know what to say. The longer that I looked at her, the tighter my stomach clenched and the stronger I felt drawn to her. She still had that something. She still had that inexplicable, beyond definition quality that she had had in high school. I hadn't had time for her then. I barely even acknowledged her, even when I hadn't been able to stop thinking about her. She had been too quiet, too withdrawn. It didn't fit in with the popularity that I had so carefully constructed. Now I felt like I was getting another chance. I had another opportunity to be close to Charlotte and maybe get to know her. But she didn't know who I was. She didn't even know who she was. I felt a powerful pull to her and a desire to protect her and guard her, not just from what was happening now but from what had led her into the storm.

"What have you been cooking up?"

It was all that I could manage, but I looked at the food that she had piled onto the counter, so I could look fully invested in her nocturnal culinary adventure.

Charlotte laughed and stood up from her chair, walking over to me and surveying the food.

"I don't even really know," she said. "I woke up starving and all of this looked good. I didn't really think it all the way through."

I laughed, relieved to hear a hint of lightness in her voice. I looked through everything and pulled out a few things, putting them aside, and then put the rest away.

"How about this?" I asked.

Charlotte looked at the eggs, bacon, bread, and butter that I had kept out, her mouth twisted to one side as she scrutinized it carefully, making a show of putting her finger to her chin and considering the options. Finally, she nodded.

"Looks like a plan," she said.

"Perfect."

I noticed her looking around the kitchen and realized that she hadn't gotten as far as finding the pots and pans, so I gestured toward one of the cabinets. She opened it and pulled out a cast iron skillet. There was a brief moment when it seemed a bit touch-and-go, as though the heavy metal pan was going to get the best of her small frame, but she rallied and placed it on the stove. We were silent for a few moments, falling into what almost felt like a comfortable pattern of preparing the food. She opened the package of bacon and spread several strips in the pan, then turned to look at me.

"How long have you lived here?" she asked.

"A few years," I said.

She nodded.

"Do you live alone?"

Her voice had the tone of being forced casual, like she didn't want me to think that there was anything more to the inquiry than just simple curiosity. I knew, though, that if the situation was reversed and I had found myself in her house, I would have asked the same thing. I would have wanted to confirm that I wasn't going to be surprised by a boyfriend or husband trudging his way home through the snow. I nodded.

"Yes," I said. "Always have."

"It's a big house for you to be living here all by yourself," she said. "Why did you come up here to the middle of nowhere?"

I felt myself bristle involuntarily.

This was why. So that people wouldn't be around to question me or my motives.

I fought against the angry response, telling myself that Charlotte had nothing to do with what had happened. She wasn't a part of it. Even if she hadn't lost her memory, she likely wouldn't know what I had gone through or what had motivated me to come up this far. She didn't strike me as the type of woman who devoted herself to college football or who would have given a second thought to the news about a player's leg being crushed by a drunk driver smashing into the back of his car and sending it spiraling into a retaining wall. The news outlets were eager to latch onto the story, to sensationalize it and emphasize the tragedy of my destroyed career. I couldn't even count the number of times that I heard that my crushed leg had crushed my dreams. This was only the beginning. The stories had faded by the time that my world completely fell apart.

"I made my money in software and technology," I said, falling back on the reasoning that I had used so many times before. "I made enough from the sale of my company and the programs that I had been working on that I invested and now have more than enough to keep me going for far longer than I'm going to survive. I didn't really see much point in continuing to work a job that didn't give me any satisfaction for more money that I didn't need. So, I built this lodge, came up here, got Scout, and..."

"The rest is history?"

"Well, not yet. But it will be."

I was surprised at how candid I was able to be with her. Since the last moment that I saw Helen, I wasn't one to open up to or trust anyone. She had torn that out of me. It was only a matter of a few weeks later that I watched the last flickers of life disappear from my mother, removing from me any remaining traces of desire to be around people. Cold and angry, I wanted nothing more than to be alone.

Now, though, that had changed. In an instant, I felt myself drawn to a person like I hadn't been in so many years. If I was honest, it was more than I had ever been. Even Helen, the woman I thought would one day be my wife, hadn't been able to crack fully through the walls that protected me, that guarded me from the darkest moments of my past, moments that continued to linger on even years after I was out of danger. I didn't want to let myself feel it. Charlotte was only here for a few days, if that. When the storm was gone, she would be, too.

Charlotte opened two drawers and then found a fork in the third. She used it to pull the cooked bacon out of the pan and rest it on a folded paper towel. I saw her notice the jar that I kept sitting beside the kitchen sink and she picked it up. I started to explain what it was to her, but she picked up the skillet and poured most of the grease into the jar. She settled the skillet back onto the stove and glanced over her shoulder at me.

"I wish I knew why I did that. It was just automatic."

I shrugged.

"Whoever taught you to cook must save bacon grease. That's what my mama always did, so that's what I do."

She cocked her hip slightly and looked off into the distance, then shook her head.

"I don't ever remember cooking before, so I don't know." She sighed and reached for the bowl of eggs that I had beaten. "That's seriously going to take some getting used to."

"What?"

"Not knowing anything. Well, knowing things, apparently, but not knowing what it is that I know."

She stopped, her expression showing that she realized just how confusing she sounded and had decided that she was going to stop while she was ahead. The eggs sizzled in the remnants of the bacon grease still in the skillet and she stirred them until they pulled together into fluffy scrambled eggs.

"Well, hopefully you won't have to get too used to it. Your memories could come back any time."

We filled plates with the eggs and bacon and I popped a fresh hot piece of toast on each before we went back to the table and settled into chairs. We fell back into the strangely comfortable silence for a few more seconds before Charlotte lifted her head at me again. She opened her mouth to say something, but then looked back down at her plate and poked at the eggs with the tines of her fork.

"What?" I asked.

She shook her head slightly and then looked at me, an indecipherable emotion in her eyes.

"Do you think that anyone's looking for me?" she asked.

The question landed with a dull pain in my chest. I could feel the worry and hesitation coming off of her.

"Do you want them to be?" I asked.

She took a bite of bacon and chewed it slowly as she thought about the question.

"I don't know," she admitted. "I was running. Does anyone who's running really want someone looking for them?"

The question hung in the air and it seemed we both tried to ignore it.

"So," I said, pushing the conversation forward, "this would usually be where I would start asking you questions about yourself, but since you wouldn't be able to answer them, do you want to just make things up?"

Charlotte picked up her toast and took a bite out of the corner.

"Yes," she said.

"What's your middle name?"

"Esmerelda."

"What do you do for a living?"

"Traveling gypsy fortune teller for weddings and bar mitzvahs. Clearly."

I chuckled.

"And do you have any pets?"

"A zebra named Fruit Stripe."

"All very good information." She smiled at me, but her smile faded into a yawn and her long, thick lashes drooped. "You should probably get some more rest," I said.

"Um...would you mind if I took a shower?" she asked.

"No. Go ahead."

She stood up and carried our plates to the sink, glancing at me as she headed for the entrance to the kitchen.

"Do you want to take one first? I wouldn't want to take all of your hot water."

I shook my head.

"It'll be fine. Go ahead. The closet in the bathroom attached to the guest room should have everything you need. I put your suitcase by the dresser if you didn't see it."

"My suitcase?" she asked.

I nodded.

"It was the only thing that I could find when I went back to the car after bringing you here. It didn't look like there was anything else in there with you. Except for the back half of the car."

"Thank you, again."

I nodded, going to the sink to rinse the dishes and tuck them into the dishwasher. Maybe I'd actually have a whole load to wash tomorrow.

Chapter Seven

Charlotte

I followed the same path back through the house to the guest room and found a suitcase sitting beside the dresser just like Micah had described that it would be.

My suitcase.

I had to try to remember that. These were my things, even if I had no memory of them or personal attachment to them. They were the connection that I had to the life that had taken an apparent detour when I crashed into the tree. I thought about that as I picked up my suitcase and brought it over to the bed to open it. The storm outside was severe and I couldn't imagine that it had gotten that intense in just the brief time that I had been in the house since Micah found me. That meant that it was probably already storming when I was driving down that road and ended up against the tree. Why would I have done that? What could possibly have been so bad that I would have run away from it into a raging snow storm?

I opened the suitcase to reveal a hastily thrown together pile of clothing. Either I had packed my things as quickly and haphazardly as I had apparently driven down the road, or I had just uncovered an interesting and not necessarily desirable character trait. Digging through, I found what would pass as the most appropriate pajamas considering I was in the home of a stranger.

A gorgeous male stranger who I might not be able to trust myself with if wearing anything less appropriate.

As I stepped into the bathroom attached to the guest room, I was stunned by how beautiful the room was. Micah was sexy in a rugged, almost wild way and I wouldn't have expected such luxury from him. I ran my fingertips along the marble countertop and remembered what he had told me about the money he made with his software programs. I was impressed by my surroundings and eager for the promise of a shower. I felt somewhat grimy, and a soreness I could only imagine caused by the crash was starting to settle into my joints and muscles. I turned on the shower, delighted to see several streams of water spring from the walls to create a surrounding rainforest effect, and stepped in. The hot water poured down my skin, relaxing my muscles and soothing a chill that I hadn't even been aware of before it slipped away. I had found a toiletry bag in my suitcase and I used the sweet-smelling body wash and shampoo to wash away the grimy feeling. As my hands ran across my skin, I couldn't get my thoughts away from Micah and the shiver that rippled through my body each time I felt his eyes on me. My eyes drifted closed and for a few seconds I imagined that it was Micah's hands that were on me, gliding across my skin, stroking my body.

My eyes snapped open and I rushed through the rest of my shower, hastily getting out and drying with one of the plush towels that I took from the closet. I got into my pajamas and swept my wet hair up and onto the top of my head to keep the chill from the back of my neck and shoulders. I walked back out into the lodge, but found it still and quiet again, just as it had been when I first emerged from the bedroom after waking. I followed the same path that I had the first time I explored the house, but noticed something that caught my eye as I moved through the great room. A curtain that had been hanging over what I had assumed was another large window was moved slightly to the side, revealing that it had actually been blocking a door. I walked toward it, wondering if Micah had maybe gone outside with Scout and worrying that they could be in danger in the storm.

I paused just outside the curtain, hesitating before I took hold of the side and moved the curtain the rest of the way open. The door led to a short slate walkway that crossed a deck and led to what looked like a small glass building. The glass walls were steamed so much that I could barely see through them, but the wall to the front was only partial, a gap of a few feet allowing me to glance inside. My breath caught in my throat as Micah stepped out from behind part of the wall. The building was an outdoor shower, the stream created by the hot water pouring from a shower head positioned on the far wall. The snow had lessened but was still swirling through the air, surrounding the shower. Despite the flakes that glittered in the glow coming from a light positioned on the eaves of the house and the moon, Micah was standing in the shower, his delectable body naked beneath the water. I felt my body tense, a spark settling between my thighs, and my mouth watered. Micah had been sexy while dressed, but now that I saw what had been hiding beneath his jeans and long-sleeved thermal shirt, he was irresistible.

Micah had been standing sideways, but now turned his back to me, leaning back slightly and running his hands down his chest. My eyes trailed along the muscles of his back and onto his strong thighs. I wanted to stand there and watch him, but couldn't let him catch me staring at him. It hadn't been an accident that he chose the isolation and solitude of the outdoor shower rather than any other that I was sure was inside the lodge. I doubted that he would be happy to find me staring at him from behind a curtain. I stepped back into the great room and let the curtain fall back into place. I turned around and saw Scout standing in the doorway to the room, looking at me as if he knew exactly what I had been doing.

"Don't tell him," I said as I made my way quickly back through the room and toward the bedroom. "Remember I'm the one who gave you bacon."

I heard the little clicks of his nails on the floor as he followed me back into the bedroom, waiting just long enough for me to climb under the covers to hop up and curl into what was becoming his customary spot. I slipped out from under the covers and rushed across the floor to close the door most of the way so that just enough light came through that I could see the bed. Almost as soon as I got back into the bed and rested my head on the pillow, I heard the muffled sound of a door closing and realized that Micah had come back inside. I imagined him walking through the lodge with a towel wrapped around his hips and I bit my bottom lip, rolling over and burying my head in the pillow. I thought again about the reality of what I was going through. I was closing my eyes again, leaving myself alone with thoughts that were appearing in a mind that didn't really know what to do with them. I had no sense of context for the actions that I took, the things that I said, or even the food that I had chosen in the kitchen. I had no sense of self. But again, I couldn't determine if that was a good thing or a bad thing. Did this mean that I had lost myself or that I was being given a rare gift -- the opportunity to create something new? Micah had said that I would likely recover my memory sometime soon. Did that mean that I got to discover myself and choose the elements that I wanted to keep, to create a truer version, an expression of who I really was?

My mind drifted away from my lack of memories and returned to Micah. I couldn't deny the attraction that I felt for him. It was powerful and intense, something so much more than I should feel after such a short time. But it felt so real. It was entirely unexpected, and yet it felt as though it had always been there.

Thoughts of Micah were with me when I fell asleep and they were with me when I opened my eyes again in the morning. For a brief moment I lay still, orienting myself again as I gradually let my thoughts creep into the back of my mind to see if they would discover any memories there. There was still nothing before the moment that I awoke in the bedroom the day before, unless I counted the flickering familiarity that I saw in Micah's eyes. I glanced to the bottom of the bed to see Scout, but there was only the impression of his warm, furry body in the comforter. I had lost my bed companion. Out in the lodge I heard what sounded like a muffled voice and knew that Scout had gotten up to join Micah. I freshened myself up and walked out into the great room, following the sound of Micah's voice until I found him coming in from outside. He was talking to Scout in an enthusiastic tone, riling the dog up until he was jumping and spinning around at Micah's feet.

Micah was wearing several layers of thick clothing, but my cheeks still burned with the memory of what I knew was underneath them, what I had seen the night before when he was showering. Snow coated his shoulders and hat, and he stomped his feet on the mat to shake off a layer from his boots. He hadn't seemed to notice me, but as he unwound the scarf from around his neck, he glanced up.

"Hello," he said.

"Good morning."

"Did you sleep well?"

"I did, thanks."

"There you go. Something you remember."

His tone was stiff and unyielding, and if I hadn't seen his fingers absently running over Scout's head while he said it, I likely would have thought that he was being an ass. Instead it seemed like it was another moment of humor, a touch of lightness coming through the cold, distant exterior. I wish I could understand what made him that way. He seemed so detached. There were moments when he was present, when he was right there with me and I felt like we were existing in a closed space only we inhabited. Within seconds, though, he changed, and I felt like I had been locked away from him. Even in those moments, though, I could sense something in him that was caring and protective. I found it intriguing, making him even more attractive.

"Don't get your hopes up too much," I said. "That's it."

"So, still Esmerelda?" he asked.

It took me a few seconds to remember what he was talking about and I nodded, trying to maintain a straight face.

"It seems so."

"Well, then, Queen of the Gypsies, if that's the case then you probably already know that the weather outside has gotten even worse. It seemed to have calmed down a little last night, but then it picked back up again and is now pretty bad. You definitely won't be going anywhere today. It might be a while until we're able to get you down the mountain. I contacted the rangers and they said that the emergency services units have been slammed since the storm started and don't know when they're going to be able to get up here."

I felt strangely upset by the revelation. He was trying to find a way to get me out of his house. The instant I allowed that thought to go through my mind, I wanted to chastise myself for being so ridiculous. Of course, this man was trying to find a way to get me down the mountain. I was a stranger who he had found crashed against a tree in a snowstorm. Helping me was his goal from the beginning, not keeping me. The voice in the back of my mind, though, said I was glad the rangers couldn't come. I wanted to spend more time with Micah. Being in the lodge with him, even in the moments when he felt closed up and cold, I felt safe in the lodge with him and the powerful pull was enough to make me want to explore more.

"OK," I said.

I had wanted to come up with something else, a quip or something at least moderately interesting, but that was all that I could manage. I wondered if I was always like this or if there was ever a time in my life when I had been articulate. This man managed to leave me stumbling over my words more times than not.

"I just came in for a few minutes to grab another cup of coffee. The storm is worse than I had anticipated and there's some more work that I want to do around the property in case it keeps going. You're more than welcome to make yourself at home around here. Relax. Watch some TV. There's a library in the back if you want to read. I'll be in and out throughout the day and Scout will be here with you. He likes some snow, but this has gone beyond his threshold."

I chuckled and patted the dog on the head as he looked up at me with an expression that almost looked like he fully understood what Micah had said and was confirming it. We walked into the kitchen and he went to work making coffee. The smell was rich and full, making me immediately wanted a cup.

A discovery.

"Can I have a cup?" I asked.

"Sure." Micah gestured at one of the cabinets. "Grab a mug."

I leaned my back against the counter and Micah did the same. We sipped our coffee in silence. I couldn't determine if it was a comfortable silence or if it was a silence that stemmed from neither of us knowing what to say. Maybe we didn't want to say anything. When he finished, Micah rinsed his mug and put it in the dishwasher with our dishes from the night before. He looked at me for a moment, then turned away and left the house. I took my last few sips of coffee and then followed his lead with the mug. I contemplated making something for breakfast, but the meal that I had eaten with Micah in the middle of the night still had me satisfied, so I decided that I would take Micah's invitation and make myself at home in the lodge. That meant doing some exploring.

I roamed through the rooms that I had already visited the night before, taking my time to notice more of the beautiful, luxurious details. The home was pure masculinity but with a sophistication that only came from someone who not only had but was accustomed to money. Yet the way that he had talked about making his money in technology and software made me feel as though that wasn't always the case. He didn't strike me as someone who grew up with wealthy parents or the world sitting at his feet. He worked hard now to take care of his lodge and the land around it, and there was the sense about him that he had worked just as hard before, if in a different way.

As I walked through a new portion of the house I began to notice the occasional decorative elements. Though luxurious, the lodge was rustic and minimal, the heavy furniture, throws, and rugs making up the majority of the accessories in the home. Every so often, however, I noticed little touches that stood out against the stone and dark wood. Bronze wall sconces accentuated one hallway. One simple painting punctuated the expanse of a wall. A cut crystal bowl, empty on a table at the juncture of a corner, the most unusual and seemingly out of place detail. As I looked at them I wondered if these were really there because he had chosen them when designing his home, or if someone who he cared deeply for, maybe the mother he had mentioned only briefly, but who had obviously been extremely important to him, had chosen these for him and he left them there in their honor.

The thought of curling up with a book sounded wonderful and I roamed through the house looking for the library. I found myself in a back hallway and I peered into the various rooms that I passed as I walked down it. All of them were open except for one. I turned the doorknob, curious about what could be in the room, but it was locked. I shook the doorknob.

Why did people do that? Was there ever a time when shaking a locked door actually caused it to open?

Feeling guilty for wanting to get into a room that Micah obviously wanted protected, I left the room and made my way down the rest of the hall and around the corner. As soon as I turned around the bend I found the open, arched doorway to the library and stepped through into a room that was richly appointed and overflowing with books displayed in tall cases and stacked on tables. I turned on the light to add to the wintery glow from outside and began to explore the titles of the books, searching for one that appealed to me. Part of me hoped that something in the titles would reach out to me and spark something, give me some sort of further insight into myself, but nothing looked familiar. I found an interesting title and took it over to one of the large chairs sitting beside a fireplace. I looked at the fireplace, wishing that it had a roaring fire to complete the ambiance. I was just giving up on that thought when I noticed a small switch on the side. I flipped it and the fireplace burst to life. The realization that Micah, the rugged outdoorsman who was currently out in a blizzard making sure that his lodge and property were protected from damage and prepared for further severe weather, had installed a gas fireplace in his library made me laugh. It was unexpected and seemingly out of character, but at the same time seemed to speak to the affluence that had crafted the rest of the lodge.

Feeling a cozy boost from the warmth and glow of the fire, I wrapped myself in a champagne-colored chenille blanket and curled into the chair. Scout had been sauntering along beside me since Micah went outside and now stepped in front of the fireplace to settle down in the warmth for a nap. I opened the book in my lap and soon lost myself in the story that unfolded on the thick pages.

"I see you found my deep, dark secret."

I looked up and saw Micah standing in the doorway. Scout looked up at him as if he was contemplating getting up and going to Micah obediently, then let out a sigh and rested his head down again. Apparently, he had had enough of the winter weather and wasn't eager to even look like he was volunteering to go out into it again.

"The library or the fireplace? Because if it's the library, you didn't conceal it very well."

I still had the fluttering in my chest that came each time that I looked at him, but I was starting to feel more at ease and like I could talk to Micah.

"I meant the fireplace."

"It is rather shocking. I would think that all of your fireplaces would require you to chop down a tree or two."

"Well, most of them do. And I try to use downed trees as much as I can rather than taking down new ones."

"How environmentally aware of you."

Micah made a sound somewhere between a chuckle and a snort and stepped further into the room.

"I'm more aware of the possibility of a tree falling and hitting other trees and eventually knocking something over so that it crushes me. It's not like there's a lot of people up on the mountain to come to my rescue. And I love my dog and all, but Scout is no Lassie. He'd probably run for help, forget five minutes later, and end up trying to play with the squirrels."

"Does he do that frequently?"

"More often than you would probably like to think."

I laughed, closing the book in my lap so that I could focus entirely on him. His eyes touched the book briefly.

"Good book?" he asked.

I looked at it and nodded.

"It is." A thought came to my mind and I looked up at him again. "So... speaking of deep, dark secrets."

Micah looked somewhat suspicious.

"Yeah?"

I hesitated. I didn't want him to think that I was prying or that I was overstepping my bounds, but the curiosity was getting the most of me.

"When I was walking around the house, I noticed that there's a locked room on this hallway."

"There is," he said.

"Um...what is it?"

As soon as I asked it, I wondered if the question was actually a good idea. What if I really didn't want to know what was behind that door? What if it was something devastating or horrifying? What if I had just done the exact thing that people yell at the vacant-minded women on true crime shows for doing and was about to get dragged into some sort of mountain retreat-meets-torture chamber? My breath had gotten more shallow and faster as my thoughts came faster and faster, quickly getting out of control.

"Do you want to know?" he asked.

I had expected that he would be more mysterious, even elusive about it, but he wasn't. I couldn't decide if that was reassuring or if it was just confirmation that this was going to go badly quickly. My eyes slid over to Scout. He was still sleeping. He wouldn't betray me, would he? A dog that sweet and calm couldn't possibly belong to a rabid serial killer, could he?

The dark place shows up quickly when you're stranded in the middle of nowhere in the snow.

"Do I?" I asked.

There was a tremble in my voice that I wasn't proud of. Not that I had any context, but I would hope that I would have a few more survival instincts in me that would make me at least somewhat more courageous in this type of situation. He shrugged and started out of the room. I thought only briefly before furthering my somewhat disturbing lack of self-preservation by getting up and following Micah out of the library. I heard a deep, beleaguered sigh behind me and then the click of Scout's nails on the floor as he followed. I stepped out into the hallway and found Micah standing just outside the locked door, holding a key in his hand.

"What do you think's in there?" he asked.

"I really have no idea," I said.

He stared at me for a few seconds and then turned toward the door.

"Let's find out."

Micah unlocked the door and stepped aside so that I could enter the room first. I felt him lean in just enough that he could hit the light switch to turn the light on in the room. As soon as I saw what was there, I felt ridiculous for my fear. I turned around and looked at him, opening my hands out to indicate the room around me.

"Really?" I asked. "This is it? Why would you keep all of this locked up so mysteriously?"

Micah shrugged and stepped further into the room, looking around as I had.

"These are the most important things to me," he said. "Other than Scout, of course."

I looked down and saw that the dog was staring at Micah, and if I hadn't known any better I would have thought that he did seem to look somewhat disdainful, as though his beloved human had just implied that he didn't matter.

The dog has become another person. Cabin fever is officially kicking in.

"What is it, exactly?" I asked.

I turned around in the center of the room slowly, looking at the shelves, shadow boxes, and displays that filled the space.

"It's my memorabilia room," he told me. "I used to play football."

There was a hint of nostalgia and a soft veil of sadness in his voice and I knew that there was more to this room than just a place where he could keep mementos of his glory days or displays of his devotion to a particular team. I walked around the room slowly, taking in all that was displayed. There were items that I might expect to be in the man cave of a sports fan. I saw shelves filled with books about the sport, replicas of awards, and photographs of Micah with players. There were other items, however, that seemed far more exclusive. I noticed footballs on stands that were autographed by multiple people, framed jerseys that held not just the name of the players who had worn them but stains and hints of damage that indicated that these had been worn during games, and other items that I couldn't imagine would be accessible to anyone other than the extremely wealthy. I couldn't understand why these things would matter so much to Micah, especially so much to create the emotion that I had heard in his voice.

The more that I looked, however, the more that I began to notice the items in the room that related directly to Micah. I noticed a display case that held a jersey from a college team as well as a variety of awards and recognitions. A pair of well-worn cleats sat on the bottom with a black scrapbook.

"Did you play all through your college years?" I asked.

Micah shook his head.

"No."

He didn't offer any more and I continued through the room. As I moved deeper into the room it seemed that I was going back through the years of Micah's life. I left his college career and found myself standing in front of two sets of shelves hanging on the wall that contained what looked almost like a shrine to the years that Micah had played football in high school.

"This is impressive," I said, amazed by the sheer volume of items that were crowded onto the display.

A framed jersey with Micah's last name emblazoned on the back was on the wall in between the two sets of shelves and the displays that bordered it contained everything from rows of trophies to ticket stubs. I saw framed newspaper clippings, several scrapbooks, score sheets, and another football positioned on a claw-shaped display.

"Most of it is my mother's doing," Micah admitted. "I was her only child. She was proud."

"It looks like she had plenty of reason to be," I said. "You seem to have made quite a name for yourself."

I stared at the jersey again, my eyes tracing the outline of the mascot on the sleeve. Something tingled in the back of my mind. There was a feeling like thoughts or emotions that I couldn't quite reach. The familiarity of Micah's eyes came back into my mind. I felt like there was something that was connecting me to the objects in front of me. Something drew me to the mascot on the jersey, the black bird against a purple and black background. I stared at it, focusing on it with all of the intensity that I could muster, determined to understand the impression that I had that these things mattered to me, that there was something significant about them that linked me to them, and to Micah. I lifted my hand to run my fingertips along the outline of the bird.

"The Ravens," Micah said. "That was the high school that -- I went to."

There was a strange hitch in his voice when he said it and I glanced over my shoulder at him. He seemed to be looking around me rather than at me, his eyes tracing the objects on the display as well. There was a question in the back of my mind. I could feel it. I knew that it was there, but I couldn't hear my own voice in my head, I couldn't hear the words or bring them forward to ask him.

Chapter Eight

Micah

I watched Charlotte exploring the display of my high school football days with tightness in my chest. I felt like my breath was caught in my throat, but I didn't know what I was supposed to do. The way that she was standing there, her eyes locked on my jersey, it seemed that she was starting to remember something, or at least was feeling a connection to what she was seeing. I didn't know what to do. I couldn't decide if I should go ahead and tell her who she was, or if I should continue to allow her to explore and see if she could figure it out on her own. My knowledge of concussions and the consequences that they could have for the person suffering one didn't go so far as to tell me what could happen to a person who had lost their memory if someone else forced them to confront who they were and what they had gone through. While I had heard of people being coached about their memories and encouraged to remember or accept what was told to them about their pasts, I didn't personally know what kind of affect that could have on a person. I didn't want to think that I could cause her any damage, but more than that, I knew that there was truly nothing that I could do for her if she thought that she was starting to remember.

As much as I still felt the intense draw to Charlotte and had an attraction to her that felt as deep and real as anything that I could have felt for someone I had known closely for years, the reality was that Charlotte and I didn't know each other. The moments that we had exchanged glances or existed just on the perimeter of each other's lives were barely tangible. They weren't enough to give me any real insight into her as a person, and they certainly didn't tell me anything that she had gone through, especially in the years that followed high school graduation. It shouldn't be my responsibility to try to reintroduce her to herself, and if she asked me, there was nothing that I would be able to tell her. I felt if I gave her even the smallest hint of who she was that she might want more and there was nothing more that I could offer her.

Before I could say anything to her, Charlotte reached up and took a framed document off of one of the shelves. I remembered the day that my mother had put that piece of paper in the frame. It was one of the most amazing moments of both of our lives, something that I don't think either of us thought would ever happen just a year before. Charlotte held the frame out to me and I took it, looking down at the letter.

"You got a scholarship," she said.

I nodded. The statement had been as much an inquiry, an invitation for me to tell her more about that time in my life and this letter if I wanted to. There was a part of me that didn't. This was why I kept this room locked. Though no one else came to the lodge, I still wanted all that was in this room to be protected and kept away from anyone else. Talking about the letter was just the beginning and I knew that it would lead down the path of a story that was a critical part of me, but one that I had tried with everything that I had to keep from anyone. Now I felt like there was nothing that I could do. She had asked me and in that moment, it was clear that there was nothing that I could deny Charlotte. Just looking at her made my stomach muscles tighten and my cock twitch, but I also felt the deep, filling need in my chest to protect and take care of her.

"I went into the college with the intention of playing professional football. Scouts had been watching me for two seasons and I had my choice of six different colleges. I got a full ride to play."

"Scout..." Charlotte said. "Maybe that's why you liked him. Scouts had found you and now you found your own. That's why his name stuck."

I gave a short laugh and nodded.

"Maybe. I never really thought about it that way."

"What happened? I mean, I see that there's memorabilia around here for you playing in college, but you said that you went with the intention of playing professionally and you told me earlier that you went to school for technology."

There was something in her voice that sounded like it was bordering on suspicion, as though she didn't know what to trust, but I couldn't blame her.

"I went for football," I said. "I was an undeclared major and, to be totally honest, I didn't have any concept of anything that I might do in life other than play football."

"Even after you retired?" she asked. "You couldn't think that you were going to be able to play forever."

I knew that she didn't mean the words as judgmentally as they seemed. They sounded more as though she were stunned at the idea of anyone thinking that way about their future. I wondered if that was part of who she was and how life had impacted her that was so deeply ingrained in her that even without the memories to define it, it influenced all of her perceptions.

"No, but I did think that I would be able to be involved with football for the rest of my life. I figured that I would play in college, then get into the pros. During my years playing, I'd save and invest. After I retired, I could go into coaching and consulting. After that I could keep doing appearances. My life would be set because of football. I didn't think that I needed to plan for anything else. Being undeclared meant that I could take just general classes and focus entirely on playing. I'd think of some sort of major whenever it became necessary. It turned out that it became necessary a lot sooner than I thought it would."

I could feel the emotions building inside of me and I fought to lock them up like I had done for years. As I did, the familiar anger started to creep through me, making its way up the back of my neck and tightening my throat until it was painful. But this was a feeling that I preferred. It was easier to be bitter and angry than it was to allow myself to feel the pain, sadness, and disappointment.

"Were you injured?" she asked.

I wondered if she had seen me favoring my aching leg.

"I was in a crash. A drunk driver. It destroyed my leg. I tried to recover enough to get back into shape. I did everything that I could to come back from it, but the injury was just too severe. I had to stop playing. That one moment literally changed the entire direction of my life. In one instant everything about my future disappeared and I had to try to piece it back together. When I realized that I couldn't play anymore, I was forced to come up with a new version of myself and what I was going to do. That injury changed my direction in college, but also everything that I hoped and dreamed for. To be honest, I didn't really hope and dream for much for a long time after that. I had lost too much. It wasn't just my ability to play football. It was...everything."

The image of Helen's face appeared in my mind again, but I didn't feel like talking about her. Charlotte was looking at me with softened eyes.

"I know that it must have been really hard for you to go through that, but you did get through it and everything turned out well for you. You might not have gotten to play football professionally, but you are still extremely successful. You're so young and you were able to retire and be up here in this gorgeous home. You have everything together and it seems like you really enjoy your life."

I didn't know how to respond to her. I felt my jaw set, the anger that had begun to build in me still in control.

"I have more work that I need to do," I said.

It was the end of the conversation and the announcement that her time in the room was finished. She seemed to understand that and walked past me and out of the room with Scout close at her heels. I flipped the switch on the wall, cloaking the vault of my memories in darkness. Locking the door, I put the key back on my keychain and secured it in the pocket of my coat before heading back through the house without another word. As I walked away, Charlotte's words repeated through my mind. She had said that it seemed that I had my life together, but I didn't entirely believe her. The life I was living was Plan B. An admittedly good Plan B, but Plan B nonetheless. I tugged my hat low over my ears and covered my mouth and nose with my scarf as I stepped out into the snow. The wind bit into my skin and I thought about what my life would have been like if I had been able to go all the way and play in the professional league. Would I have still chosen to devote my entire existence to football? I wondered if Helen and I would still be together. Would we have gotten married? How long would our marriage have lasted?

Charlotte's face appeared in my mind and the sound of her laugh played in my ears, and I questioned whether I would even still want to be with her. An uncomfortable realization was forming in my mind, something that I didn't want to even admit to myself because it didn't fit in with the narrative that I had used to define myself for so long, the motivation that had contributed heavily to my decision to come up here. I knew deep inside me, though, that Helen never would have been the type of woman who I would want as a wife. Other than gorgeous and available, there was little about her that actually made her appealing to me and even less appealing was the world that she inhabited. My family was decidedly lower class when I was younger, but football had acted as a stopgap measure, ensuring that I was able to move comfortably in the popular crowds. That had only increased when I got into college and the money that people's families had didn't seem to matter as much as it had in high school. By merit of my place on the football team alone I immediately made friends and started doing the weekly tour of parties and gatherings. That was how I met Helen. She quickly introduced me to a different type of party, ones that were thrown by the members of society and attended by only the wealthiest and most powerful people.

Those parties were where I learned that there was far more to having money than I had ever realized. There were many things that had appealed to me about their lifestyle, but one that didn't was the often vacant look in the eyes of the couples when they looked at each other. There were so many marriages that seemed to be built on little more than the power that their unions created and the fact that they looked good together. In the moments when I was really honest with myself, I knew that if Helen and I had actually stayed together and gotten married, we would have been one of those couples.

Charlotte was in the guest room when I finished working and turned down my offer for dinner, telling me that she had already made a sandwich and was just going to stay in and read. I thought about our interaction in the memorabilia room, knowing that I had pushed her away. The next morning, however, she was standing in the kitchen when I woke up. Her thick hair was coiled on top of her head again and I longed to release it from the clip and see it tumble down. I wanted to dig my fingers in it and feel it wrapped around my hand as I pulled it, tugging her head back to expose her soft neck as I took her.

She smiled at me from the stove as she babied an omelet and I craved her even more. I imagined grasping her ass and picking her up to set her on the counter, spreading her thighs and feasting on her rather than on the breakfast she was cooking. I barely tasted the food or felt the hot coffee that I drank. I was so wrapped up in my thoughts about her and when I finished I went directly to the door.

"I'll see you later," I said, wanting to get out into the snow and let the cold get my brain and my cock back under control.

"You have more work to do?" she asked, sounding almost disappointed, but also curious.

"There are some smaller buildings on the property that I'm planning on repairing in the spring. The wind isn't so intense today, so I want to go check on them to make sure that they weren't damaged in the storm. Then I need to tend to the smokehouses and I wanted to bring some more supplies into the emergency shelter. If this first storm is any indication, this winter is going to be rough and I might need to use it."

I was pulling my gloves on when I saw Charlotte coming toward me.

"Can I help you?" she asked.

"What?"

"I mean...could you use any help?"

"You want to help me?"

She looked around.

"I don't really want to just stay around here alone all day again," she said. "I think it might do me good to get outside."

I looked at her for a few seconds, as much surprised by her enthusiasm as I was by the offer.

"I don't know how much you're going to be able to help me. It's not exactly easy work. But if you really don't want to be here, you're welcome to come along."

Charlotte wasn't deterred, and she held up a finger.

"Just give me a minute to get dressed."

She rushed out of the kitchen and disappeared into the back of the house. A few minutes later she came back zipping her coat. She wasn't wearing a hat or gloves, and I knew that she couldn't go out in this weather that unprotected. I opened a cabinet in the mudroom and pulled out a pair of extra gloves and a thick hat. I held them out to Charlotte and she put them on, smiling gratefully.

"You look adorable," I told her. I turned and opened the door to a blast of wintry air studded with icy snowflakes. "Absolutely useless, but fucking adorable."

"Hey!" she protested as she followed me. "How do you know I'm useless?"

"I don't," I admitted. "You don't, either. And let's be honest, you're don't exactly look like you're cut out to be much assistance out here."

Charlotte took two defiant steps toward me and promptly sank down in the snow. She tried to adjust her position but only managed to knock herself over backwards, so she landed in the drift.

"Son of a bitch," she said up into the falling snowflakes.

"Perfect."

I walked back to her and reached down for her hand. She grasped mine and I yanked her up to her feet. The pull made her stumble toward me and I felt her body hit my chest. My arms wrapped around her waist and for a moment we stood pressed together. My heart was pounding in my chest and I felt my desire for Charlotte spike higher. My mouth was watering as I started to duck my head, but she took a step back from me. I shook my head to get myself back into the moment and we started across the property toward the cluster of small buildings that stood several hundred yards from the original house. When I had first come up on the mountain and saw that house, I had considered moving into it just as it was, but that felt too much like I was running away. I had already spent too much of my life dealing with things because I had no other choice. I dealt with the cruelty of my father and the disdain of his family. I dealt with the lack of money and struggle when he was finally gone but my mother was left to raise me on her own. I dealt with the agony of recovery and trying to regain what had been taken from me when that driver smashed into me. I dealt with the dreams I had carried for so long being taken away from me. I dealt with Helen's betrayal. The one thing that I would never say that I dealt with was my mother's death.

In all of those situations, I had no choice. There was nothing that I could do but figure out ways to deal with what I was going through, even if I didn't accept it. But when I moved onto the mountain, I had a choice. I was in absolute control and I was going to exert it. I designed the lodge and ensured the contractors were compensated handsomely for making sure that it was completed at breakneck speed so that I could move into my new home and start a life that was truly my own.

I was happy to see that these buildings, which I intended to have fully repaired and preserved come spring, had weathered the storm well. Since they were currently employed as storage sheds, the materials needed to mend the few small patches of damage were close at hand and I went to work. Charlotte took the initiative of watching what I was doing and then repeating it on another section of the home to repair a section of wood that had been torn loose. I followed behind her to finish the job, but was impressed by her willingness to dive into the project and to learn so quickly.

"Maybe you're a carpenter in real life," I said with a laugh.

"I don't think so," she said.

"Why not?"

"Not enough blisters on my hands. Besides, I think that if I did this with any frequency, I would be a lot more ripped."

I laughed again, and we continued working. Though I had always valued the solitude of the mountain, that afternoon I found myself enjoying having Charlotte with me. The snow had lessened until it was barely falling and together we crossed off every item on the list of work that I knew I needed to do. There were other things that I could have done, but I knew that I had come up with those tasks purely as a way to keep myself busy and away from the temptation that was Charlotte. When she shivered and looked longingly toward the house, however, I knew that I wanted to be back inside with her. She was shaking when we got back in and I felt guilty for keeping her outside as long as I did. I doubted that she was wearing enough layers to really protect her from the cold and I should have made sure that she was more ready before tromping her through drifts that sometimes hit her hips.

"Go take a hot shower," I told her. "I'll make some cocoa and have it ready for you when you get out."

"Cocoa?" she asked, one eyebrow raised. "That's manly."

"It's dark cocoa."

Charlotte let out one of her intoxicating giggles and headed toward the room that I had begun to think of as hers. I went into the kitchen and took out a pot. Setting it on the stove, I went to the refrigerator for the milk and cream. I didn't need a recipe. The process of making the cocoa that I had gulped by what felt like the gallon when I was younger was deeply ingrained in me. I could probably have done it in the dark. There was a sudden scream of wind from outside and I glanced up at the light fixture, wondering if there was a possibility that I would be doing it in the dark. As the milk and cream heated, I crossed the kitchen to pantry and took out the rest of the ingredients. Soon the room filled with the heady smell of chocolate, a smell that always managed to make me feel comforted. Yet in that moment all I could think about was how that chocolate would taste if I licked it from Charlotte's skin.

I was so lost in the thought of my tongue sweeping a drop of the hot chocolate from the valley between Charlotte's hips that I wasn't thinking when I reached for the handle of the cast iron pot. The heated metal seared into my skin and I snatched my hand back, hissing as I shook it, trying to cool it in the air.

"Mother fucker!" I shouted.

Scout rushed to my side as I grabbed my wrist and gritted my teeth against the pain of the burn. I walked over to the sink and turned on the cold water, putting my hand beneath it.

"What happened?"

I turned around and saw Charlotte standing in the doorway to the kitchen. I had to turn my hips back toward the sink to hide my quickly hardening cock as it strained against the front of my pants at the sight of her. She wore only a towel wrapped around her, the top low enough to see the upper swells of her breasts and the bottom revealing a few inches of her thigh. Her wet hair hung around her face and down her shoulders, but she hadn't yet washed away her makeup. The effect was intensely sexy, and I could barely contain myself.

"I burned myself," I told her, trying now to concentrate on the pain rather than my arousal.

"Let me look at it."

She rushed up to my side and took my hand from under the water. She cradled it in one of her palms and I felt the warmth of her skin against mine.

"It's fine," I told her.

"You should still put something on it," she said. "Where's your first aid kit?"

I directed her to it and she guided me back toward the kitchen table. I sat in the same chair where she had sat her first morning in the lodge while I remedied the cut on her forehead and allowed her to gently dry my hand. She dipped her fingers into burn salve and rubbed it into my skin. Her breath seemed to become deeper as she touched me, and I noticed a slight flush cross the swells of her breasts. The pads of her fingers swirled over my hand for several seconds longer that was needed to coat the burn, but I didn't want her to stop. She was leaning close to me and I could see the beads of water from her shower slip over her collarbone and down between her breasts. My hunger for her swelled in my belly and I couldn't resist it any longer. I leaned forward and swept my tongue between her breasts, collecting the drops of water and bringing them into my mouth with the taste of her skin. Charlotte drew in a shuddering breath and I reached forward to take hold of her hips. My fingers pressed into her skin through the towel and I pulled her forward toward me, drawing my tongue up between her breasts again.

I felt Charlotte's hands rest onto my shoulders and for a moment her fingers pressed into me just as mine were into her hips, but then I felt her push away and take a step back. She didn't look at me, but tightened the top of her towel and started toward the door.

"I should go finish my shower," she said. "It's getting cold."

She rushed out of the room and I resisted the urge to let out a growl. I wasn't used to feeling this way. I didn't think that I ever would again. After Helen, I shut down that part of myself, not wanting to deal with the frustration and anger that came from trying to maintain a relationship. But now I couldn't get my mind off of this woman, a woman who had first caught my attention, so many years before and now didn't know who she was. I wanted her like I had never wanted anyone before, but I didn't know how to reach her, or if she would have ever given me the time of day if she did remember.

Charlotte again spent the rest of the evening in her room. I couldn't sleep that night and found myself walking quietly into her room to check on her, ensuring that she was sleeping peacefully. I felt a strange, cold tension in the air when I woke up the next morning. I decided to pretend that the night before hadn't happened. As much as it was killing me not to touch her, I didn't want to scare her. It was more important to make her feel safe and secure. I was in the kitchen when she walked in. It seemed that this was becoming our customary meeting point and she crossed the room with familiarity to fill a mug with coffee. I liked that she was starting to feel comfortable, but I had to remind myself that this wasn't the way that it was going to be soon. When the storm was over and the mountain was less dangerous, she would be gone. The radio sitting on the counter crackled slightly as another warning came over the waves. I tensed just as I had every time that happened since finding Charlotte. I was waiting for them to announce that she was missing or that her family was looking for her. When I talked to the rangers they hadn't had anyone report a woman missing on the mountain and even after I directed them to her car, they made no mention that anyone had requested the car be recovered. I couldn't understand why no one would have reported that she was up on the mountain and hadn't returned, or that her car hadn't been seen. Was it possible that no one had noticed that Charlotte was missing? Or did someone know that she hadn't returned, but not think it was important to let anyone know? Neither option was particularly encouraging. It meant that if I hadn't found her, it was likely that no one would have. In this weather, she wouldn't have lasted for long.

The thought of the announcement eventually coming through the radio, though, wasn't something that I looked forward to. I knew that when it did, I would have to tell her that it was for her and I didn't know how she would react.

"Happy Thanksgiving," I said as she took her first sip of coffee.

"It's Thanksgiving?" she asked, looking surprised by the revelation.

I nodded.

"I don't really do the whole feast, but I'm going to roast a chicken and warm up some vegetables."

"That sounds delicious."

She was looking at me now and I didn't see the hesitation from the night before. Instead, there was curiosity and hunger in her eyes.

"I watch football on Thanksgiving," I said.

Charlotte shrugged.

"I don't know what I do on Thanksgiving, so watching football sounds fine to me. You'll have to explain the game to me. I don't think that I know anything about it."

I smiled at her and nodded.

"I can do that."

Her tongue slipped out and glazed across her bottom lip.

"I'm going to go back to the library for a while and finish that book." She walked to the door and glanced back at me. "Call me if you need me."

It took all of the control I had not to follow her, but I let her disappear into the hallway and then went to work putting together our makeshift Thanksgiving dinner. Two hours later she walked back in, a smile on her face as she smelled the air.

"Are you hungry?" I asked.

She nodded.

"It smells wonderful in here. Thank you for doing this."

"Not a big deal," he said. "I'm not into the whole idea of the pathetic bachelor subsisting on nothing but frozen meals and boxes of meal helpers so I learned to cook."

I held a plate out to her and then filled mine with the food I had made. I picked up a napkin and carried the plate and a beer into the living room. Charlotte followed and settled onto the opposite end of the couch.

"Is the game on?" she asked.

"Yeah. I hope you don't mind eating in here."

She shook her head.

"Not at all."

I turned the game on and within minutes it was clear that she really didn't know anything about the game. Whether this was another layer of her memory loss or a hint at her interests in life before the crash, she seemed completely lost. I eased closer to her on the couch and gestured at the TV.

"I'm rooting for the ones in blue," I said.

"Alright," she said with a nod. "I will, too."

I laughed and started to explain each step of the game with her. It was the first time that I had talked about football with anyone in years and I found myself enjoying it much more than I thought that I would. Rather than the sadness that I had become accustomed to feeling every time that I turned football on, this game felt different. Suddenly it didn't feel as though I was watching something that I had lost, but rather like I was helping her to discover something new. I delighted in watching her as she stared intently at the TV screen, trying to reconcile what I was telling her with what she was seeing. There were several times when she glanced over at me, her beautiful face contorted with a look of confusion, and I had to remember that she didn't understand some of the terms that I was using. I would go back and explain it to her in better terms, and Charlotte would nod. I didn't know if she was actually interested in what she was watching, or if this was just something that she was doing because she really didn't have much else choice, but I enjoyed having her there with me.

We were in the second quarter of the second game of the day when it became clear that the novelty of watching football head worn off and Charlotte was beginning to get bored. She had stopped asking questions and instead was just curled in the corner of the sofa staring out of the window and occasionally glancing over at me.

"We don't have to watch this anymore if you don't want to," I said.

"It's alright," she said. "I know that this is your Thanksgiving tradition and that you love football. I wouldn't want you to stop on my account. We can keep watching."

"It's fine," I told her. "My team is losing pretty badly anyway. I don't particularly want to devote the next couple of hours of my life to watching them get stomped. We can do something else."

"What did you have in mind?"

Her eyes slid over to me and I saw a smirk on her lips.

"Do you want to play a game?"

My stomach clenched, and I felt my lips curl up into a smile.

"Sure."

Well, shit. She actually meant a fucking game.

"How is it that you have no memory, but somehow you're able to play a board game?" I asked.

Charlotte shook her head, shrugging as she looked over the game board she had set up on the table in front of us. I had barely even remembered that I had a stack of old games in the library, but she had emerged carrying the Clue game with a delighted, excited expression on her face and I knew that I couldn't turn her down. This was nothing like the game that I wanted to play with her. I wasn't much interested in finding out who had murdered the mysterious Mr. Body in any of the rooms of his nonsensically designed Mansion. I would much rather be exploring Charlotte's body in every room of my lodge.

"I don't know," she said. "It's just kind of there. Maybe I didn't lose all of my memory. My brain just decided what it wanted to hold on to."

"So, you think that you have selective memory loss and your brain decided to keep cooking eggs and how to play Clue."

"Apparently."

I laughed and reached for the die. I rolled, landing on one for the third turn in a row. Charlotte laughed as I picked up my game piece and set it down sharply on the next square. She rolled and ended just beside me.

"Hi," I said.

"Hi."

I picked up the die and rolled again, finally creeping into the room in front of me.

"I suggest that it was Colonel Mustard in the drawing room with the revolver."

Charlotte checked the cards in her hand and held out the drawing room card.

"What is a drawing room, anyway?" she asked.

"I thought you would know something like that," I said, jotting the clue down on my paper.

"Why would you say that?"

I realized what I had said, and my mind went blank. I didn't know what to say. Now didn't seem to be the best time to just slip 'because you come from one of the wealthiest new money families in the town where I used to live' into the conversation. Finally, I shook my head.

"Just something about you," I said.

Charlotte looked at me strangely, then looked at the door to the hallway.

"I'm getting hungry again," she said. "Is there any dessert?"

"There's a pumpkin pie," I told her. "It's just one of those frozen ones. I might be able to pull together a halfway decent dinner, but my skills draw the line at baking."

"That sounds amazing. I'm going to go get a piece." She walked to the door and then looked back at me. "Do you want some pie?"

Dear lord, you have no idea how much I want pie right now. I'll make sure yours has plenty of cream.

Chapter Nine

Charlotte

I thought about watching the football game with Micah as I dished out huge slices of pumpkin pie and carried them back into the library where we had set up the board game. His face had changed as we sat there in the living room watching the game unfold in front of us. It had brightness, some of the darkness and severity that I had seen in it disappearing as he told me about the rules of the game and explained each of the plays to me. I could see the love that he had for the game and could only imagine how passionate he must have been when he played. Something about him talking about football had stuck with me, prickling in the back of my mind like the look in his eyes and the black bird on the football jersey in his memorabilia room. It was like a flash of a memory that I couldn't quite touch. It went through my mind so quickly that I couldn't even concentrate on it long enough to really know what it was that I might be remembering. The more that I thought about it, however, the more I worried that it wasn't really memories at all. It was entirely possible that I wasn't actually remembering anything or even getting close to remembering anything, that it was the desperation of my mind trying to cling to anything that might seem familiar. I wondered if it was possible that my mind wanted so much to remember things that it had started to make up these supposed memories, the sense of familiarity to give me some sense of identity, a past, and a place in the world.

As I walked out of the kitchen holding the slices of pie my eyes flickered over to the chair where Micah had sat at the table the night before. My heart pounded, and the insides of my thighs trembled as I thought of his tongue touching my skin. I'd been nearly overwhelmed by the touch, not knowing how to respond to it. Even though I wanted nothing more than for him to touch me more, I had run away from the situation, the moment that it was threatening to make me lose all control.

I handed Micah his plate and curled up into the chair beside the fireplace where I had sat to read. This was quickly becoming one of my favorite places in the house and I wanted to spend as much time in it as I could. I took a bite of the thick, spicy pumpkin filling and a sense of nostalgia surrounded me. It was a purely sensory memory, but it was something that I knew, something that was concrete and familiar. I looked at Micah and watched as he took his first bite, the expression on his face telling me that he felt the same emotional reaction to the flavor. I felt more connected to him in that second. It seemed so strange and almost ridiculous for me to feel that way, but the sense of distance between us seemed to lessen and the connection that was growing between us, the powerful attraction that I couldn't deny, intensified as I realized that we had this shared knowledge, this shared memory.

"Tell me more about when you used to play football," I said.

I didn't know how he was going to react to the question and I hoped that it wouldn't make him upset. He had seemed so happy when we were watching the game and I wanted to see more of that sparkle in him, and learn more about that part of his life. Even though he hadn't played in many years, it was obvious that the time that he had spent on the field was incredibly formative for him and I wanted more insight into what had crafted this extraordinary man in front of me.

"It was something that I always wanted to do" Micah told me without hesitation. "I don't even remember when I started wanting to play. It's like it was always a part of me. I tried out for the high school team as soon as I was allowed too and made JV for my freshman year. I was on varsity for the next three years. It didn't just feel like a sport to me it was like it was a part of me, like I didn't know who I was without football. If someone had told me that I would grow up and not be able to play anymore, there's no way that I would have believed them. I would have told him that there was absolutely nothing that would have kept me from a field. I truly believed then that I would have to die in order to not play anymore." He gave a short, mirthless laugh. "I guess that's just part of being a teenager. You think that you're invincible. You don't understand that the world around you is just one big bitch and eventually it's going to come up and bite you in the ass."

"You did everything that you could to keep playing," I tried to reassure him. "It's not like you just gave up."

"I know. But that doesn't make it any easier. I think that's why I was able to be a successful in my career as I was. I was so angry."

"Angry?" I asked. "Angry that you couldn't play?"

Micah nodded.

"Angry that I couldn't play," he agreed. "Angry at the man who was stupid enough to get drunk and then get behind the wheel of a car. Angry at the car itself. Angry at the world around me. Angry at myself."

I stood up and put my plate on the table before crossing to Micah. I leaned down and nuzzled the tip of his nose with mine. I wanted to comfort him, to reassure him. He tilted his face toward mine and I felt his lips. That first brush of our mouths against one another I felt as though it could have been an accident, but it instantly fueled Micah forward. His mouth captured mine and his tongue touched my lips, coaxing them to part so that he could explore my mouth. I complied, opening my mouth and welcoming his tongue in to tangle with mine. The kiss was hungry and passionate, the culmination of the intense draw to him that I had felt since the first moment that I saw him. I had stepped forward, wanting to settle into his lap and further the kiss, when there was a loud popping sound and the lodge went dark.

I gasped and jumped back from Micah involuntarily. There was a moment of pitch blackness before my eyes became accustomed to the small amount of light that was still coming through the thick curtains that hung over the windows. Micah muttered a profanity and stood, gently pushing me out of the way so that he could go to the window and open the curtains. The light from outside had the almost searing brightness that came from reflecting off of the snow and I squinted, turning away from it to give my eyes a chance to adjust yet again.

"Shit," Micah said. "I was afraid that this was going to happen."

"Does this happen very much?" I asked.

"No," he said. "But the storm was so severe so quickly that I knew there was a possibility. Give me a minute, I have emergency lanterns around here somewhere. I keep them in almost every room, so I don't have to search around for them if this happens."

I could hear Scout whimpering and I looked around for him.

"Is he alright?"

"He's fine," Micah said. "He's just frightened. He'll go curl up around the wood stove and hide there until the lights come back on."

I watched as Micah moved around the library, trying to remember where he had stashed the lanterns. The way that he was searching made me think that the lanterns weren't something that he had initially thought of when coming to live in the lodge. Instead, he probably purchased them as a response to the last time that the power went out. He finally found two lanterns and brought them over to the table, putting them beside the game board. Despite the intensity of the sunlight that was coming through the windows, I knew that the sun would be setting soon and very quickly the house would get dark.

"There's a generator for the refrigerator and freezers that automatically turns on," he said. "But I'll have to go activate the one for the lights."

"Don't go out there," I told him. "If the power went out, that means that the storm is getting worse and I don't want you outside."

"It's fine," he said. "I only have to go a short distance."

I shook my head.

"I don't want you to go outside. There's plenty of light right now. We will be fine."

"The sun will be down in less than an hour," he said.

"Then we will be fine in the dark."

My heart pounded slightly in my chest as I said it, but I tried not to let my expression show what I was feeling. I could still taste his kiss on my lips and feel his fingers on my hips. Almost as though it were in response to what we had said, the light coming in through the window started to fade. Micah turned on one of the lanterns and gestured toward the Clue board.

"Do you want to keep playing?" he asked.

I nodded. I didn't really know what I wanted, or what I should want. I had no memories of ever feeling this way before, and something told me that even if I could remember every single second that I had lived, I would know that this was different. I would know that I had never experienced what coursed through me every time that I looked at Micah and that was only getting stronger and more irresistible with every passing second. The heat between us was growing. It was obvious, hanging in the air around us and filling the space until it was almost as though I could feel each breath streaming out of my lungs and entering his, only to be returned to me. But I didn't know what to do with those thoughts or feelings. I didn't know how to respond or even what would happen if I did allow myself to give into the desires that filled me. I didn't want to play, but the hesitation and nervousness were enough to bring me to sit back at the table and pick up the die, after moving my plate.

"I think it was Miss White in the drawing room with the rope."

"Seriously?" Micah asked.

I thought that Micah was upset that I had started to play again, but then realized that he was sifting through the cards in his hand. He pulled a card from his deck and flashed it at me. I let out a sigh.

"Stop showing me the damn rope!" I laughed.

It was at least the fifth time that he had shown me that particular card and we were making almost no progress in the game.

"Well, stop choosing it as your weapon."

We had each taken two more turns when I stared out over the board and sighed. The sun was completely set, leaving only the lanterns to illuminate the board. It gave a decidedly eerie touch to the game, but I could barely concentrate on the stalemated mystery.

"I feel like we're going around in circles here," Micah said in response to my obvious frustration. "One of us should have figured it out by now. I don't really remember games running on like this when I was a kid."

"Maybe playing with just two players wasn't the best idea," I admitted.

"Maybe having an imaginary player that has a bunch of cards that we don't get to see isn't the best idea," he said.

I nodded.

"Valid."

There was a quiet moment and I looked up to meet Micah's eyes. The tension that had been steadily building between us had only been slightly lessened by the kiss and now it surged forward until I felt like my chest was going to burst with the pounding of my heart.

"Maybe I'll take one more turn," Micah said.

His voice had taken on a slow, deep tone that sounded like velvet and I felt my skin shiver. Micah stood and walked around the table so that he was behind me. He got down on his knees and pressed his body to the back of my chair as he reached around me. I nodded, and Micah took the die from my hand, his fingertips lingering as they ran along my palm. His mouth brushed along the side of my neck as he rolled the die and moved his game piece to a corner of the board that didn't have a room.

"I think that it was Professor Plum in the bedroom with..." he reached across the gameboard and picked up the red game piece. He dropped it in place beside his own purple piece, "you."

I turned my head and immediately Micah's mouth captured mine. Our kiss was instantly deep and seeking, pushing through what we had discovered the first time that our mouths met toward the powerful, aching potential that waited just beyond. I climbed to my feet and Micah took both of my hands, pulling me closer to him. He wrapped his arms tightly around my waist as I clutched either side of his face. Micah plunged his tongue into my mouth. When our lips parted, we moved simultaneously toward the door to the library. Micah snatched the lit lantern from the table as we went, providing just enough light for us to follow as we stepped out into the hallway. I stepped out first and started down the passage toward my bedroom. After walking a few feet, I felt Micah grab the back of my shirt and pull me so that he could push my back against the wall and crush his mouth onto mine again.

We kissed passionately for a few seconds and then Micah pulled away from me, continuing on his way down the hallway. I followed, suddenly mimicking Micah's action by grasping his wrist and turning him around. He complied with my gesture, but immediately took control again, taking my hand so that he could press me to the opposite wall. He reached down and interlaced his fingers with mine, lifting my arms so that he could hold them against the wall on either side of my head.

I leaned forward to touch my mouth to the side of Micah's neck and kissed along the tight band of muscle there, enjoying the way that his pulse felt beneath my lips as it quickened and drummed against his smooth, warm skin. Micah moaned softly at the kiss and then turned his head, using his forehead to push my head back against the wall. He took over my gesture now, kissing his way along my neck and down to the neckline of my shirt where he ran his tongue across my skin. He suddenly released me, and we started down the hallway again, our steps quickening as we turned and wound our way through the massive lodge toward my bedroom. We were nearly there when he turned and took me by the front of the shirt with both hands, yanking me up against his body and turning so that I was pressed against the wall again, his body enveloping mine as he pushed me back with the weight from his shoulders to his thighs. His hips nudged against mine and I gasped as I felt the hardening bulge at the front his pants. I could feel his tongue come out to glide along my collarbone and then dip down into the soft hollow at the base of my throat. I tilted my head back to give him greater access to my skin.

After several seconds Micah pushed back off of me and took me by the hand, pulling me away from the direction of the bedroom where I had been sleeping and toward another part of the house. We made it to a set of steps that led up and we started up them. Micah turned and sat on one of the steps, pulling me forward until I straddled his hips. He pressed me down onto him, kissing me until I felt breathless and reaching for the bottom of my shirt. I released the grip that I had around his neck to allow him to peel my shirt off and toss it to the side. He wrapped one arm tightly around my waist and used the other hand to grasp the back of my head, leading me to lean back so that he could press his face into my breasts. His tongue slipped out again and I felt the same intoxicating feeling that I had the night before. I gasped as his tongue swept between my breasts and then beneath one cup to flicker across my nipple. My hips rocked against his involuntarily and I heard Micah groan, grabbing me by my butt to lift me off of his lap so that he could stand. He started up the steps again and I followed him.

As soon as we stepped through a heavy wooden door into a massive bedroom, Micah turned and gathered me into his arms again. I knew that we were on an inevitable path, one that we had started on from the moment that I first saw Micah, and the nervousness started to creep into the edges of my mind again. Micah seemed to sense it and pulled back just enough to look into my face.

"What's wrong?" he asked.

I held Micah closer to me in an effort to reassure him.

"It's just..." I said.

"It's just what?" he asked.

I hesitated for a moment. I was unsure of what to say, but I knew that I had to say something.

"I don't know if I've ever done this before. I can't remember being touched by anyone."

Micah tucked his hands around my jaw and stared into my eyes.

"Do you want me to touch you?" he asked, his voice low and grumbling in his throat.

"Yes," I said.

"Do you want to know everything that I've wanted to do to you since the first time that I looked at you?"

I drew in a breath.

"Yes."

"Let me show you."

I felt my stomach clench and Micah's erection harden even further, seeming to strain toward me through his pants. Without another word, he tilted his head for another kiss. I felt stronger and more confident now, and willingly offered myself over into his hands. As we continued to kiss, Micah guided me backward toward the bed. When I felt the mattress on the back of my thighs, I sat. He lowered to his knees in front of me, pressing my thighs apart so that he could get between them and draw close to me. Micah flattened his hands on my chest and ran them down toward the waistband of my stretch pants. He followed the touch of his hands with a trail of open-mouth kisses from my shoulder down my chest and belly. My stomach trembled when Micah's mouth reached my navel and the tip of his tongue dipped into it.

Micah's breath was a blend of temperature against my skin, cool against the dampened trail that he created and warm against the other areas. The contrast was intoxicating, and I found myself lifting my hips toward Micah almost involuntarily. He reached around behind my back to release my bra, slipping it down my arms and away from my body so that my breasts were bare. His hand ran along my waist and onto my hip before moving into the apex of my thighs. The touch was subtle, but it felt like a shock of electricity moving through my body. Micah tenderly but insistently massaged into the warm dampness of my center, only increasing my arousal so that I ached with need. Micah sat back and pulled off his shirt, then rose up on his knees so he could kiss me again. I felt the warmth of his chest brush across my breasts and I reached out to touch it, finally indulging myself in the feeling of his chiseled muscles and his skin on my fingertips.

As we kissed, Micah's hand moved up to my waistband and he joined it with the other so that he could ease my pants down my hips and off of my legs. I was fully bare now, and I felt Micah's eyes roaming along every inch of my body that he could see. I had been able to feel the hunger in those eyes before when he looked at me, but now he wasn't just looking at me. He was touching me, tracing my body with his fingertips rather than just his gaze, offering me everything that had hovered in those heated moments between us, surrounding us but just out of reach.

Micah drew my bottom lip into his mouth and sucked it possessively. I replied by bringing his tongue into my mouth and his lips left mine to touch my cheek, then made their way onto my jaw and down the side of my neck. The progression was torturous, but I didn't want to miss even a moment of it. Micah's tongue found my nipple and he paused there, concentrating on the taut peak for a few moments while his fingertips replicated the attention on my other breast. He continued down and soon I felt his tongue dip into my navel again. My body was trembling with anticipation although I was unsure of what each step ahead would bring, I was nearly overwhelmed by the need to follow him as he guided me.

I reached down to run my fingers through Micah's hair as he kissed his way from my navel to the apex of my thighs. His hand slid up the inside of my thigh and suddenly his fingertips slipped into the tender petals of my core. I bit down on my lip to muffle the gasp that built up in my chest and squeezed my eyes closed. I could feel Micah's breath teasing the sensitive pearl at my peak and then the wet heat of his tongue slid up through my folds. I drew in a breath and Micah seemed to release the control he had been maintaining since guiding me to the bed, opening his mouth fully so that he could close it over my center.

His mouth was skillful and attentive, moving over my most sensitive curves and dips with just enough suction to make my body tingle and my breath escape from my lungs in desperate pants. I felt him touch one finger to my entrance and an instant later it slid fully inside. His hand picked up the rhythm of his mouth so that he stroked inside me while his mouth continued to suck and lick along my clit and folds. After a few seconds he added another finger and brought his mouth up, so he could concentrate all of the movements of the tip of his tongue on the tight bud he had coaxed forward with his masterful attention.

I pulled myself back up to a reclining position so that I could see Micah. I watched as his hand left the mattress besides me and ran it along his own belly. It slipped beneath the waistband of his pants and pushed it out of the way to reveal his thick cock. I groaned as he wrapped his hand around his mouth watering length and began to stroke himself in the same pattern that he continued with his fingers inside of me. I felt myself rushing headlong toward oblivion but just when I thought I wouldn't be able to hold off any longer, Micah took his mouth away from me and sat back on his heels. I watched as he stroked himself a few more times, his eyes focused on my wetness and his fingers enveloped within me. Finally, his eyes lifted to mine and he licked his lips, gathering my shimmering fluids from them.

"More?" he asked in a husky whisper.

I kept my hand at the base of his head and ran the pad of my thumb across my lips. I wanted to respond, but I could only nod. Micah had stood and pushed his pants the rest of the way off, kicking them aside so that they tangled with mine on the floor. The sight of our clothes piled together was oddly intimate and I felt an irresistible desire to touch Micah. I reached forward and tucked my hands around the back of his thighs, applying gentle pressure to guide him closer to me. He positioned himself between my thighs and I flattened my hand on his belly to feel the muscles twitching there. I looked up at him with questioning in my eyes. Micah pressed his hand to mine and guided it down his belly until it reached his erection. Keeping his eyes locked on my face, he guided my hand to wrap around his shaft until I held it in a tight grip.

I drew in a breath and followed the pressure of Micah's hand as he taught me to stroke him. After a few moments he pressed his hands to my shoulders and toppled me backwards onto the mattress. He stretched his body across mine and covered my mouth with his own. I hungrily sought his tongue and groaned into his mouth as he rocked his hips, stroking his impossibly thick, hard cock against my belly. I could feel the slick fluids forming at the tip of his erection, allowing our skin to glide across each other easily as the sensation built. We kissed passionately, inhibitions falling away if we offered ourselves fully to what was happening between us.

Micah ended the kiss and backed off of the side of the bed so that he knelt between my legs again. I thought that he was going to run his tongue up through my folds again, but I was surprised by him flattening his hands on the backs of my thighs and pressing my legs up and apart. He paused for a moment, blowing a stream of cool air against my heated skin. Then I felt his mouth touch my opening and I let out of strangled cry, sitting up sharply in response to the dizzyingly pleasurable sensation. He used one hand to press me back onto the mattress and the other to lift my hips slightly so that he had better access for his eager mouth.

I couldn't withhold the moans that his mouth inspired. I closed my eyes and relinquished myself to the intense feeling of Micah's skillful, attentive touch and felt myself opening further beneath his tongue. My legs were shaking and sweat with beating on my chest when he gave a final lick that traced up to my clit again. I opened my eyes and saw Micah stand.

"Slide back," he said breathily.

I did as I was told, sliding backwards on the bed so that I was lying with my head on the pillows. Micah climbed up onto the bed with me, positioning himself in between my legs and tipping forward to plant his hand on the side of me so he could look down into my face. I felt his thick and impossibly hard erection nudging at my opening and I lifted my knees slightly. Suddenly I noticed his eyes darken and he gritted his teeth, mumbling something beneath his breath. He scrambled off the bed and I felt a sinking feeling in my belly. I sat up, reaching for the blanket that was spread across the comforter so that I could cover myself. Then I noticed that Micah was going to his dresser, opening the top drawer. He turned around and I saw a box of condoms in his hand.

"I didn't think that I would ever going to use these," he said.

"Then why do you have them?" I asked.

I didn't really understand why, but it bothered me that they were there.

"I guess it's just something that I learned when I was younger and never really grew out of it. But I'm glad that I have them now."

He opened the box, which I was glad to see was new, and pulled one of the foil packets out. Tossing the rest of the box back into the drawer, he stood at the end of the bed and tore the packet open with his teeth. I watched, my mouth watering, as he took the condom from the packet and settled it onto the tip of his erection. He held the base of his shaft with one hand and rolled the condom down gradually. When it was finally in place, he crawled back up onto the bed and I lay down again, resting my head back onto the pillow and opening my arms to him. He settled over me and I felt the tip of his cock edging at me again. He reached down and touched the deliciously sensitive place again. He placed his fingers in his mouth and then return them to my opening, allowing the warm wetness to soften me further, preparing me though I already knew I was wet and hot beneath his touch. I felt him ease inside my body and I tightened around him. He rose up over me again supporting himself on his knee as he brought his mouth down to my ear. Micah lightly kissed my neck.

"Relax," he whispered. "Let me take care of you."

I willed my body to relax. He continued to nudge forward with his hips gently, gradually increasing the pressure as I submitted to the feeling allowed my body to open. He wrapped one hand around the base of his cock and the other on my hip to hold me steady and my body gave in and welcomed him fully. I groaned as Micah filled me, giving me a sense of fulfillment and wholeness that I couldn't describe.

His hips immediately began to move. My body continued to open and relax as Micah's cock stroked within me, and I reached down to touch where our bodies melded. I lifted my head to lick the sweat off of Micah's shoulder, indulging a sudden desire to sink my teeth into his straining muscles. I heard Micah growl at the bite and he increased his pace for a few intense strokes before pulling out of my body. There was a brief moment of emptiness and disappointment before Micah grabbed me by my hips and flipped me over onto my belly.

I felt Micah's thighs on either side of my hips before I felt his cock sink inside me again. The new angle was even more intense, and I buried my head in the pillow to muffle the cry that bubbled up from my throat. Micah supported himself on one hand beside me and slipped the other beneath my throat to lift my head up toward him. His mouth ran along my neck, leading up to my ear so that he could nip my earlobe with his teeth. I whimpered as Micah pushed deeper into me and held in place so that the sensations built to a nearly overwhelming pitch.

"I've been waiting for this," he whispered into my ear. "I've wanted you since the moment I saw you."

"Me, too," I murmured.

Micah turned my face toward his for deep kiss as he rocked his hips harder and faster. Soon his grunts became rhythmic and he pounded into me possessively. There was something intimidating about his intensity, yet it also felt thrilling and empowering. I lifted my hips slightly and felt Micah give a final, impaling thrust as he growled deep in his chest. His cock throbbed inside me and I could feel him spilling within me. I gasped, lifting my hips further to slide a hand beneath my body, grasping Micah's and leading it down to the apex of my thighs so that he could bring me relief from the pressure tightening through the muscles of my hips, thighs, and stomach. Almost as soon as he touched me, however, Micah pulled out of me and flipped me back over onto my back. He moved my hand out of the way and replaced it with his own. The pad of his thumb massage into my clit hard and fast. When I was panting and holding onto the covers beside me so tightly my knuckles ached, Micah leaned down and enveloped my desperate core with his mouth and sucked it deeply. I roared as I felt the pressure shatter in a mind-blowing orgasm pour out into Micah's mouth.

Micah moaned luxuriously and traced me slowly with his tongue, occasionally dipping it inside of me to feel the spasms of my walls. I arched up off of the mattress and let out another trembling cry before dropping down and gasping for breath. Micah slowly brought his mouth away from my entrance and kissed his way along my inner thigh, then on to my belly and up until he was resting on top of me. We kissed languidly as our bodies calmed and cooled, and our heartbeats slowed. I buried my fingers in Micah's hair and ran the other hand along his back. Finally, he slid to the side and sat up to pull the blanket from the end of the bed up over us. Turning off the lamp he settled beside me again. I rolled to the side and tucked my head into the curve of his neck and shoulder, breathing in the warm, musky smell of him until sleep overtook me.

Chapter Ten

Micah

"How'd you sleep last night?" Charlotte asked as she came into the kitchen the next morning.

The power had come back on at some point during the night and I was brewing our customary pot of coffee. As I turned to look at her my jaw dropped. She was wearing nothing but one of my flannel pajama shirts, and only three of the buttons were buttoned. I could see enough of her body beneath it that my cock began to stir. I knew that last night wasn't enough. One night with her was nowhere near enough to satisfy the hunger that I had for her. The first time that I let my lips touch her skin memories of aching for her when we were in high school came back and only worked to intensify the almost animalistic needs that I had for her.

"Pretty well," I told her. "How did you sleep?"

"Like a baby," she said. "But I didn't like waking up without you in the bed beside me."

"Did you miss me?"

Charlotte nodded and stepped forward. She tucked her fingers into the belt loop of my jeans and leaned in to lick the side of my neck. I let out a murmur and touched my hands to her hips. I guided her backward toward the kitchen table, but before the backs of her thighs could touch the chair, I turned around and sat down.

Without me even having to give the suggestion, Charlotte lowered down to her knees between my legs and ran her tongue across my collarbones. I had grasped onto her wrists and I could feel the trembling of her heartbeat beneath my fingertips. I gave her a hard tug to pull her up against my body and she groaned at the feeling of my rapidly hardening erection pressing into her belly. Our mouths met and tangled in an intense, but brief kiss.

When our lips parted, Charlotte brought hers to the side of my neck and began to work her way down in a trail of kisses until I felt her mouth brush over my nipple. The peak tightened beneath her lips and she drew it between her teeth. I hissed, but made no move to try to push her away. Pressing one hand to the opposite side of my chest, she continued down until she was kissing her way along my belly. She didn't pause to get any acknowledgement from me before bringing both of her hands to the front of my belt and releasing it. I had only gotten so far as to put on my jeans that morning, but now I wished that I wore even less as she worked her way into my pants.

The taste of Charlotte on my tongue and the feeling of her on my lips was intoxicating and I craved more. I didn't care about anything that had happened before I found her. I didn't want to think of anything that would happen when the snow stopped. All that mattered was now.

My cock sprung out of my pants and Charlotte wrapped her hand eagerly around it. She licked her lips hungrily and then leaned down to draw her tongue along the slit at the very tip. She looked up and I looked down at her. The slumbering in her eyes told me she was trying hard to maintain her control, but I knew that I wanted her to lose it. As though she had heard my thoughts and wanted the same for me, she opened her mouth and welcomed the entirety of my length inside across her warm, sweet tongue. The feeling was delectable and dizzying, and I wanted much more.

Charlotte tightened her hand around the base of my erection and used it to hold it still as she let her mouth begin to glide in a fast, intense rhythm. She occasionally added deep sucks, bring the tip of my cock further into her mouth and toward her throat. Sitting back on her heels, she started twisting her hand and drawing it up and down using short strokes to complement each glide of her mouth. She suddenly paused and ran her tongue along my shaft, as though she were focusing on the feeling of every vein and ridge. I closed my eyes, trying to commit the feeling to memory so if ever there was a time that I longed for her I would be able to bring this sensation to mind. I no longer tried to control my reactions to the sensations that Charlotte was creating with her mouth and I accompanied my loud, rhythmic groans with a dig of my fingers through her thick hair, grasping at the back of her head to both encourage and control her movements.

I clamped my hand down on her shoulder and began to thrust into her mouth. I felt Charlotte relinquish herself to my control and allow me to express my increase in passion with each rock of my hips. My sounds were becoming deeper and more insistent, and I knew that my climax was rushing forward. I tightened my grip on her hair and felt Charlotte's fingertips press into my thighs as though not to give me the opportunity to pull away. She continued to suck, seeming to express as much of a need for me as I felt for her as she whimpered and moaned with every deep draw of my cock into her mouth. The tip touched the back of her throat and I growled, lifting my hips up off of the chair. My head fell back, and I let out a growl as I felt my cock tighten and then throb, releasing a thick, smooth stream across Charlotte's tongue. I held her in place and slowed my thrusts, then lowered my hips to the chair as she drew her mouth along my length at a more leisurely pace, swallowing luxuriously and cleaning me with her tongue.

She climbed to her feet and smiled down at me. Her fingers touched the buttons on the front of my shirt that she wore and slowly began to release them.

"I think that maybe I should go take a shower," she said.

"Oh, really?" I asked, standing.

I kicked out of my pants and trunks so that I stood naked in the middle of the kitchen. The rush of the orgasm was still flowing through me, but just seeing Charlotte standing there, her hair loose and wild around her face and shoulders, moving with torturous slowness as she revealed her skin to me, was enough to start my cock twitching to life again.

"Mmmm-hmmm," she said, biting into her bottom lip and nodding as she took a step back.

She had released the buttons now, but my shirt still hung closed, concealing far too much of her body. I closed the space between us and reached up to push the shirt off of her shoulders. The cooler air touched her skin and I saw her pert pink nipples harden. Growling, I swept her up and over my shoulder, running out of the room and through the house. Her sweet, round ass was sticking straight up in the air and I reached up to give it a slight little smack as I approached the door in the great room. I opened the door and Charlotte squealed as the sharply cold air from outside swept over her naked body. I hit the switch on the wall before leaving, turning on the shower.

I ran along the short walkway toward the partially outdoor shower, hissing as my bare feet touched the icy slate. Steam was already billowing from the shower and the ground around it was warmer. I lowered Charlotte to her feet inside the shower and backed her up so that we both stood beneath the hot water. She moaned happily and tilted her head back to let the water stream through her hair. It poured down her shoulders and over her breasts, making her skin shimmer. I reached up and took a bottle of body wash from the cabinet attached to the inside of the wall. Filling my palm with the gel, I rubbed my hands together to create a thick, white lather. I reached for her body and let my hands run along her skin. The sight of the bubbles trailing along her belly and into the apex of her thighs, nestling into her folds, brought my cock to full length and hardness and I immediately dropped to my knees in front of her. Grasping her leg with one hand, I swept it up so that it rested over my shoulder. This opened her to me and I could feel the enticing heat of her body.

I lapped at her ravenously, plunging my tongue into her and tasting her fluids as they flowed, preparing her body for me. Charlotte's legs were shaking, and I could feel her arching as I licked her relentlessly, letting the tip of my tongue slide up through her folds and focus directly on her clit. It emerged from its hood, revealing the most tender and sensitive of her tissues, and I eagerly lavished more attention on it. Charlotte's hands delved into my hair and I felt her tug on it as she screamed out and came into my mouth. I stood and reached into the cabinet again, pulling out one of the condoms that I had tucked onto the shelf earlier that morning before Charlotte had woken up. I held it up for her to see and her mouth opened in surprise.

"You planned this," she said.

"Baby, I've been planning this for..." *years...* "a long time."

I went to open the package, but she took it out of my hand and tore it open. Most of the lather that I had spread on her body had been rinsed away while I worshipped her, but there was some still on her belly and she gathered it onto her hands. Reaching forward, Charlotte wrapped one hand around my cock and stroked it. I thought that I was fully hard, but the touch of her soft hand engorged me even further. She pulled the condom from the package and rolled it into place, then wrapped her arms around my neck and brought her mouth back to mine.

As I closed my mouth over hers in a deep kiss, my mind went back to that football game so many years before. I could see her sitting in the stands again, everything else faded around her. I don't know why she was there. I don't remember any other time that she had come to a game, and I never noticed her there again after. It was entirely possible that she was there to watch one of the other players, one of the other guys who had a more legitimate place in her social circle. But I had seen those eyes staring directly at me. I had felt her watching me. And I saw those eyes now as she pulled back and looked at me with expectation and desire. I pulled her away from the wall and turned her, sweeping her up into my arms and pushing her back against another wall so that we were both beneath the stream of hot water again. Her legs wrapped around my waist and I sank into her. Her body accepted me more readily and eagerly than the night before and I didn't need to hesitate for even a second to begin to thrust into her at an almost frantic pace. Charlotte wrapped her arms around my head, pulling it into tuck against her chest as she cried out with each hard stroke.

After a few seconds I stopped and let her lower down to her feet. I took her by her hips and turned her around sharply. Grasping both of her hands by her sides, I lifted them up and flattened them onto the wall in front of her. I ran my hands down the sides of her body and stroked them over her ass, pulling her cheeks apart then running my fingers down until they met the dripping heat of her core. I pushed her thighs apart until her feet were nearly against the walls on either side of her, opening her to me completely. I tucked my hand between her thighs so that I could flatten my hand on the front of her pelvis and pulled back so that she took a few steps back, causing her to bend over at the waist. The water continued to fall on her back, but her hips were now sitting nearly out of the water. I grasped the base of my cock with one hand and rested the other to her lower back to stabilize her before plunging into her again.

I grabbed her hips and used them to slam into her hard and fast. My balls slapped against her and I suddenly felt her reach back between her legs to hold them, massaging them. I took her hand and led it to her clit, pressing her fingers to it.

"Touch yourself," I said. "Show me what you like."

Charlotte whimpered, and I felt her fingers beginning to move. Her fingertips stroked over her clit, occasionally slipping down to run over my shaft in between thrusts. Her knees bent slightly and the hand on the wall in front of her slid down several inches, driving me deeper into her. I could hear Charlotte rapidly approaching climax, rushing toward it as she swirled her fingers across her clit and I filled her. Finally, she screamed out and I felt what I had been denied the night before. Her walls tightened down around my cock and then the pressure dissolved into a cascade of spasms that drew me deeper into her and created even more powerful sensations through the head and along my shaft. The image of the lather rolling down her chest and onto her belly came into my mind again and I pulled out of her, turning her around and pushing her back against the wall as I yanked the condom off.

She reached forward and took my cock in her hand, joining my own tight, fast strokes until I let out a roar and watched myself come onto her belly. She groaned, biting her bottom lip as if in ecstasy. Her hand slipped away from my already relaxing erection and went to her belly, so she could trace her fingertips through the thick stream on her skin. I kissed her, cupping my hand around her jaw. For the next several minutes we carefully washed each other, taking time to explore each other's bodies, discovering more. As I touched every bit of her, letting my fingertips run along the bones of her spine and following the trail of my touch with kisses, I knew that my desire for her was far from quenched. It was as if each time that I felt her skin or tasted her lips, it refueled me, sparking my need even more. I wanted to be inside her again. I wanted to let everything disappear, just as it had when I saw her in those stands.

I brought her back to my bedroom that night and laid her down beside me to sleep. I didn't want her to sleep in the guest room again. I didn't want her to sleep anywhere else again.

****

Charlotte

I woke up curled into the curve of Micah's body. It felt warm and comfortable in his arms, and I was surrounded by a sense of safety and protection. It was as though nothing could get to me as long as I was enveloped in him. I never wanted to leave that. I never wanted to get out from under the comforter and sheets that were warmed by his body and filled with the heady smell of him. The room was still dark around me and I realized it wasn't morning. Waking up in the middle of the night felt familiar and I realized that I was having a flash of memory. I could remember getting out of bed in the middle of the night, slipping out of my bedroom and down to the kitchen to have a snack. The memory felt real, but there was a distance about it that kept me from knowing how long ago that memory was. It could have been mere days before Micah found me, or it could have been when I was just a child. Either way, it was something about me that I honestly remembered, and I clung to it. Even though I was still unsure whether I wanted to remember everything that had happened before the crash, I found it reassuring to have at least something from my past that told me I wasn't always afraid, I wasn't always trying to escape from something.

I cuddled closer to Micah so that I could listen to the rhythm of his heart through his chest. I had my hand rested on his stomach and the deep, even rise and fall of his breath was peaceful and grounding. I kissed his chest and then the side of his neck. He didn't stir, and I touched a soft kiss to his lips before slipping out from beneath the blankets. I grabbed a pair of sweatpants and long sleeve shirt and slipped them on before stuffing my feet into Micah's slippers and heading toward the kitchen. I was happy to hear a little clicking sound of Scout falling into step behind me. He wasn't allowed to curl up at the end of the bed and sleep with me and Micah, and when he looked up at me with his huge, emotional eyes, it looked like he was trying to tell me that he missed me.

"Hi, boy," I said. "Come on, let's go get a snack."

Scout's tail wagged happily, and he pranced along beside me. I felt like we were sneaking through the house, but there was something fun about it. I was starting to no longer feel like I was a guest in this place. I might still not fully understand myself, and part of me may still feel as though I was a visitor in my own body, but here, in this place, surrounded by the constant feeling and reminders of Micah, I was safe and comfortable. The subtle night lights positioned around the lodge gave me just enough illumination to get me into the kitchen without having to flip any of the switches. I opened the refrigerator and by the light of the small bulb inside explored the various containers of leftovers and other foods that filled the shelves.

"What are you in the mood for?" I asked, looking down at the dog. "Something salty? Something sweet?"

Scout stared at me and tilted his head to one side.

"You're right. We should start with something healthy. That's the only way to go."

I reached into the refrigerator and pulled out the plate of leftover chicken that Micah had carved from earlier along with a bowl of mashed potatoes and another of green beans. Balancing them all, I closed the door with my hip and walked over to the table. I was developing a particular fondness for this table. I thought about the first night I was in the lodge when I sat in this very chair and let Micah treat the cut on my forehead. The wound was so small that it was almost completely healed now, and I didn't think that it would leave a mark. In a few more days that reminder of the crash would be gone and all that I would be left with was what Micah had told me about it. I realized in that moment that I didn't even know what type of car I was driving when I crashed. I wished that I knew. It seemed ridiculous, but I felt like somehow if I knew what type of car I had been in, I would know a little bit more about myself.

"Did you see the car?" I asked Scout.

He looked at me and then his eyes drifted over to the plate of chicken on the table. They snapped back to me and he tried hard to concentrate, but then they drifted over again. I laughed.

"Yeah, I know. The important things in life."

I contemplated whether I should go to the cabinet and get another plate, but then I figured that would just mean more dishes and there was really no point in that. I peeled away the plastic wrap on each of the dishes and then picked up a piece of dark chicken meat. I held it up so that Scout could see it, then tossed it up in the air. Part of me expected that he would jump up and catch it, but instead he turned around a few times and let it bounce off of his back.

"That was masterful, Buddy."

I nibbled my way through some of the leftover breast meat and then used green beans to scoop up the mashed potatoes. I was glad that Micah hadn't joined me for my late-night snack. I don't think that I could have lived with myself if he had seen me with my makeshift utensils. There are just some things that you need to keep to yourself. When I felt that I had consumed a sufficient amount of the savory leftovers to claim that I was at least trying to be healthy, I covered them all with plastic again and brought them back to the refrigerator. I pulled out the pumpkin pie and set it on the counter. I knew that this particular leftover was going to warrant a plate and a fork. If I dug straight into the pie, it was an entirely real possibility that there wouldn't be any left by the time I was finished.

Not that self-control had been the most glowing of my personal characteristics over the last few days.

I sat back at the table and took a few bites of the pie, letting the same feeling wash over me as it had earlier. I remembered the look on Micah's face when he, too, had taken a bite of the pie and I wished that I knew more about when he was younger. Some things that he had said had stuck with me and I can only assume that there was darkness even before the crash that had taken his career, and his dreams, away from him. I didn't want to think about anything ever hurting Micah, but I could see in his eyes that it had. I felt the strange and unexplainable urge to protect him from that hurt, just as I felt that he was protecting me. I hoped that in some way I would be able to shield him from the memories that caused him pain, whatever those memories were.

I heard a sniffling sound from beside me and I looked over to see Scout staring at the pie expectantly. The expression in his eyes almost said 'aren't you going to share that with me?' I looked at my fork and then back at him.

"Are dogs allowed to have pumpkin? Is that one of those things that would make you sick?"

He just kept looking at me, so I scooped up some of the filling and let it drop to the floor.

"Oops," I said. "Look what I did."

I figured that if I pretended that it was an accident it would be more forgivable that I was dropping pumpkin on the floor and letting a dog lick it up. I'd try to remember to search around for some cleaning products and do a once-over in the morning. If Micah had to go out to do any more work around the property, I could clean up a bit for him, not that the lodge really needed much cleaning other than the sheets being washed. The thought brought an unexpected smile to my lips. I found myself enjoying the thought of him going off to do some sort of gruff, masculine work while I took care of the house for him and welcomed him back home.

Well, that will go down as the least feminist thing that I have ever thought...at least, I think it is.

I scraped the last of the pie filling from the plate, licked it off the fork, and tossed a chunk of remaining crust down to Scout. Feeling completely stuffed and finally sleepy again, I tucked the plate into the dishwasher and then covered the rest of the pie with plastic. I slipped it back onto the shelf and reached for a glass bottle of milk. I stared at the name of the creamery and wondered if it was near the mountain. I had just taken the bottle into my hand and straightened when out of the corner of my eye I saw a dark figure in the doorway, its shape silhouetted against the light from a night light in the great room. I gasped, and the milk dropped from my hand, crashing to the floor. The sound of the glass breaking sounded like an explosion in the quiet night and I screamed, startled as much by the cold milk that splashed up and soaked through my pants as I was the sound.

I stumbled back, my hand clasping at my heart as if to hold it in my chest. Thoughts rushed through my mind, racing by in a blur of colors that eventually cleared enough that I could see a face and hear a voice. I didn't know it. I didn't recognize it. But I was terrified of it.

Chapter Eleven

Micah

"Charlotte!"

The sound of the bottle breaking had startled me, but seeing Charlotte stumble back away from the refrigerator like that, had scared the fuck out of me. I hit the light switch and saw her crouched down on the floor, one hand over her heart and the other grasping the chair beside her as if trying to keep her balance. She shook her head as I approached, making my way around the glass carefully. The last thing that we needed was another injury.

"I'm fine," she said.

"You don't look like you're fine," I said. "What was that?"

"You just startled me, that's all."

"Startled you? This doesn't look like I just startled you."

Charlotte looked up at me and I saw tears in her eyes. I reached out and ran my fingers along the side of her face. She tilted it toward my touch, closing her eyes as if my fingertips on her skin could protect her from whatever she was seeing. I held my hand out and she took hers from the chair and rested into my palm. I helped her up and carefully guided her back so that she sat on one of the chairs.

"I'm so sorry about all of this," she said, looking at the mess across the kitchen floor.

I shook my head.

"Don't worry about it. It's not a big deal. I can clean it up." I crouched down in front of her and rested my hands on her thighs, so I could look into her face. "What happened?"

"I don't know," she said. "I was just taking the milk out of the refrigerator and I looked up and saw you. I didn't know who you were, and it scared me."

"You didn't know who I was?" I asked. "You know that I'm the only one here with you."

"I know," Charlotte said. I could see that she was shaking. "I know that. But for some reason when I looked up and all I could see was the shape of you standing there, I didn't know. I didn't know that it was you. I didn't know that you were the only one here with me. I felt like I didn't even know that I was here. Does that even make sense?"

I wished that it did. I wished that I can understand what was going through her mind and what had happened in the moment that she looked up at me.

"Did you remember something?" I asked. "Is that what happened?"

Charlotte seemed to stare over me for a few seconds, and then nodded.

"I think so," she said. "But I don't know what I remembered. It was so fast. Just a few flickers. Just the flash of a face and the sound of a voice. I don't even know what it was saying. But it scared me so much. It's almost like my body remembered something even if my mind couldn't."

As soon as she said it, I felt my jaw set and my head start to pound. I remembered something from high school, something that had faded away with time but that had remained in the back of my mind until this moment. I saw her young, innocent face again, the face that had captured me in the hallway and distracted me from the football stands. This time, though, that face was drawn and reddened, tears like the ones from the night that I found her in the car staining her cheeks. I didn't know what had happened in the moments before I turned the corner into the empty back hallway of the school and found her standing there like that, but I knew that whatever it was, it had something to do with the guy who was standing right in front of her.

It was one of the guys who was born into her social circle, enjoying popularity only because of his name and his money. Unlike me, he wore the tried-and-true uniform of those people. Khakis and a pastel polo shirt. It was the same look that his father probably had, and maybe even his grandfather. It was the look that meant that someone could line up a row of pictures of nearly all of the guys in his circle, clip off their heads, interchange them, and they would still look exactly the same. Unlike me.

He was standing so close to her. It wasn't unusual to see people, especially couples, close together in these back hallways when classes weren't in session. There were times when I had my fair share of girls who I stood very close to in these hallways after school when the teachers drifted their way up toward the lounge or the office and created the perfect environment for hormones to run wild. But there was something different about the way that this guy was close to Charlotte. His back was stiff, and his chest was pressed toward her as she seemed to fold away from him, withering even in just his presence. My eyes lowered, and I saw that his fists were clenched tightly at his sides.

He hadn't seen me there. If he had, he wouldn't have lifted his hand to her. He wouldn't have pressed that hand to the front of her chest and shoved her back against the wall behind her so hard that her head snapped back and her eyes clenched closed. In that moment everything that I had ever gone through and seen my mother suffer had exploded behind my eyes and the world suddenly went red. I grabbed him by the back of his shirt and wrenched him away from her. He had started to say something, but my fist stopped him. It was one punch, but it was enough to send him to the floor.

"Are you OK?" I asked her now, just as I had then when we stood in that hallway.

She shook now just as she had then, her shoulders trembling and her eyes glistening with tears that she seemed to be fighting to keep inside. Composure was something that people like her valued, I had learned. The more in control she seemed, the less anyone would pry into what was behind her pretty eyes and gentle smile.

"What if there is something horrible that I'm running from, but I'm never able to remember it?" she asked. "What If I never get all of my memories back and I never really know what happened? I might be in danger, and have no idea. How am I supposed to protect myself if I don't even know what I'm protecting myself from?"

I took her face in my hands, holding it so that she would look into my eyes.

"I will protect you," I said. "I will always protect you."

Just like I protected you then. Even though you don't remember. Even if you never remember.

I leaned forward and touched my lips to Charlotte's. I could taste tears clinging to them and I licked them away, whisking the salt away from her skin as if each tear that I removed was a bit of her pain that I could take away from her. Memories were starting to filter back into her mind, but they weren't the ones that she would want to have. They weren't the ones that I would want for her.

Charlotte's lips parted beneath mine and I deepened the kiss. My tongue swept into her mouth, brushing across hers, and I lowered my hands to her waist. I drew her toward the edge of the chair. Her hands settled on either side of my neck and she pressed further into the kiss as if she were searching for something within it. My fingers dipped into the waistband of the sweatpants she was wearing, and I pulled on them until she lifted her hips, so I could slide them the rest of the way off. Our mouths parted long enough for her to take off her shirt and me to step out of my pajama pants, then caught again. I tucked one arm under her legs, sweeping her up to cradle her against my chest as I carried her through the kitchen and into the great room. I lowered her to the couch and walked up to the fireplace. I hadn't tended to the fire that evening and it had nearly died, but I was able to encourage it back to life with the poker, soon filling the room with the light and warmth of its flames.

I put the poker away and went back to the couch. I held my hands out to Charlotte and she took them, letting me help her to her feet. Once she was standing I wrapped my arms around her and pulled her close so that our bodies pressed together. Our lips played against each other as I walked backward toward the rug in front of the fire, drawing her along with me. I lowered down to my knees, guiding her down so that we knelt on the rug, touching from chest to knee, and continued to kiss. Sitting back on my heels, I drew Charlotte forward so that she climbed into my lap. I felt the warm heat of her body cradling my erection and I wanted nothing more than to sink inside of her and feel her body, but I knew that I couldn't.

"Wait right here," I whispered into her ear.

I eased her carefully off of my lap and went to the bathroom where I had stashed several condoms. I put one on before going back into the room with her, not wanting even another second of hesitation. When I got back into the room, I knelt on the rug again and Charlotte folded into my arms, her lush body wrapping around me and her head coming to rest on my shoulder as she lowered onto my shaft. I tightened my hips to sink into her further and enjoyed the feeling of every inch gliding along her walls. Her thighs on either side of my hips kept her tight and we felt fully melded. I closed my eyes and leaned my head against hers, concentrating on the feeling of our breath and the way our hearts seemed to beat toward one another. Their rhythms started erratic, then slowed and quickened in response to one another until they were in concert. My hand pressed to her lower back guided Charlotte's hips into a slow roll against mine. I breathed her in and made everything else disappear.

****

Charlotte

I wrapped myself around Micah, giving myself over to his strength, and closed my eyes. I wanted nothing more than him. I wanted nothing but the feeling of him possessing my body and soothing an ache in my heart that I didn't understand, but that I knew was there. The flashes of memory that I had had in the kitchen were brutal, excruciating even in their brevity, and I didn't want to let them in any further. If I gave myself entirely to Micah, allowed him to fill me so completely, then even those memories couldn't reach me. There would be no space for them. In the same way, Micah seemed to be filling himself with me. The muscles in his arms strained with how tightly he held me, and he rested his head against mine as if he didn't want any space between us.

That was the way that it stayed between us for the next few days. The time blended so seamlessly, I barely kept track of how long it had been since I had come to be with Micah. We were completely wrapped up in one another, disappearing into each other as we pretended that there wasn't anything or anyone else in the world around us. We were almost desperate, using each other to numb our pain. With every moment that passed, however, I felt like the peace that we had found was running out of time. The attraction that I had toward Micah was undeniable and the powerful feelings that seemed to get stronger each day were purely visceral, but no matter how hard I tried to fight it, I had the lingering sense that Micah and this place couldn't be a part of my life moving forward. We were in a snow globe. Everything was perfection, but it was contained, it was temporary. We were stuck here for now, making the most of what we were given, but eventually it would be over, and we would have to go back to our lives. Micah would go back to the way that things were before he found me, up here alone on the mountain. I didn't know what I would return to, but there was nothing that I could do to change the reality. I was trying to fight it, but I couldn't. As much as I wanted to believe that Micah and I could discover where what was happening between us could go, I felt like there was something trying to pull us apart.

It had been nearly two weeks since the crash when I looked at Micah over the cup of hot chocolate that I was drinking.

"Is the car that I was driving when I crashed still there?" I asked.

He looked up at me, his expression as surprised as I felt to have finally asked. I had been thinking about the car and the crash itself for days and my curiosity finally took over.

"I'm not positive," he said, "but I would assume that it is. The rangers haven't announced that everything's clear yet. The second storm that blew through knocked them back even further, so I don't think they've made it anywhere close to this far up the mountain yet.

If they had, they would have announced that the tree had been moved and the road was passable again."

"So, you don't think that it's been moved?"

"No. Why?"

"I've just been thinking about it. Do you think that you could bring me to it?"

"Are you going to try to drive around the tree?" he asked.

I knew that he was kidding, but there was a hint in Micah's voice that said he was actually concerned that I was going to try to make my way down the mountain. I shook my head and laughed, reaching for his hands and bringing them up to my mouth to kiss them.

"No, I'm not going to drive around the tree. I'm just curious. I just want to see it and find out if it jogs anything. Maybe I haven't actually lost my memory, maybe it's just on pause. If I go back to the last moments before I remember anything, maybe it will hit the play button again. "

"That's an interesting theory," Micah said. "I'll take you, if you're sure that you want to go, but it's kind of a long walk. Have you ever used snowshoes before?"

I glared at him.

"If I knew whether I had used snowshoes or not, do you think that I would need a memory reset?"

"Another very valid point. Well, we're going to go with the working theory that you haven't. I have an extra pair, but there is a bit of a learning curve."

Scout came up and nudged me. I looked down at him and he wagged his tail so hard his little butt began to swing back and forth.

"Scout says that he believes in me and thinks that I'll be able to walk in them just fine."

As I watched Micah put on his snowshoes later that afternoon I had the immediate thought that it looked like he was walking around with tennis rackets strapped to his feet and I wondered if moving around in them could possibly feel as awkward as it looked. It turned out that it was exactly as awkward as it looked and felt just like I assumed it would to walk around with tennis rackets strapped to my feet. As I stumbled along through the snow toward the woods, however, I felt laughter bubbling in my chest. Rather than feeling embarrassed or uncomfortable, I was having fun trying to figure out the maneuver, and when I felt Micah reach out and take my hand to help drag me out of a particularly deep snow drift where I had gotten myself, and subsequently Scout, stuck, I had a sudden question cross my mind. Why would I think that I should be embarrassed or uncomfortable?

Micah hadn't been exaggerating when he said that it was a bit of a walk and far sooner than I would have liked, I started to feel a burn in my thighs and felt breathless. I was starting to fall behind Micah and he had to stop and pull me along. If ever there was a moment in my life when it would be appropriate to fling myself on the ground and call out 'save yourself', I figured this was it.

Determination, however, kept me on my feet and aimed toward the crash site. Finally, I saw a break in the line of trees.

"It's just ahead," Micah said. "There's a ridge that we have to go down. It's steep so you might not want to go."

"I want to try," I said.

A few moments later I stood at the top of the ridge and looked down at a massive mound of snow pressed against a tree that wore a thick layer of snow on top. Though my eyes were only seeing the white hill, I knew in the back of my mind that it wasn't actually a snowdrift. Instead, I was looking at the car that Micah had pulled me from two weeks before. I waited for something to resonate with me. I waited for anything to strike me, to jostle my mind and bring back what had happened that had left me here. It seemed like there were two parts of me. There was what I was and did before the crash and then there was what I was and did after waking up. The crash itself was the link that I thought might bridge the two, yet as I stood looking at the very place where Micah found me, likely in footsteps that he left but that were now fully covered with snow, it was like I had never been there before.

"Anything?" he asked.

I shook my head.

"How did I get from the car to the lodge?" I asked.

"I carried you."

"The whole way?"

He nodded.

The thought nearly took my breath away. This man didn't know me, he knew nothing about me, and yet he had carried me in his arms up the rocks of the ridge, and through the snow and the woods just to keep me safe. I turned to him and reached up for him, cupping my hand around the back of his head to draw his face down toward me so that I could kiss him. I wished that I could say something to him, that there were any words that could even begin to express what I felt, but I had tried that before. I had tried to thank him. It wasn't enough then and it was even less now.

"Do you still want to go down?" he asked.

I drew in a breath and nodded.

"Yeah. I want to see it."

He took my hand and started leading me down the ridge. It was slippery and steep, but by the halfway point I was more worried about Scout making it down safely than I was about myself. I stumbled a few times, but Micah was right there beside me to catch me, helping me back to my feet so that we could make our way down the rocks. Finally, my feet touched ground that was more horizontal, and I could take the few steps over to stand beside the car.

Micah had brought a stiff straw broom with him. I thought that it was an odd choice when I first saw him grab it from where it hung on the wall in the mudroom, but now I saw what had motivated him bringing it along. He walked up to the side of the car and used the broom to knock the thick layer of snow off of the top, windshield, and sides. I watched as the car came into better view, waiting for that flash of memory. He kept the snow over the back of the car, and I could only assume that he didn't want me to see what I had gone through. He reached into the deep pocket of his coat and pulled out a can of de-icer that he used on the handle to the driver's side door.

"Do you want to go in?" he asked.

I took a breath and nodded. The door resisted Micah pulling on it, but finally he managed to wrench it open and he stepped aside to gesture toward the open door as if inviting me to go for a ride. I walked up to the door and ducked down to look into the car. It was still and unassuming. The front of the interior of the cabin looked nearly perfect, as if I had just pulled up to the tree, got frustrated that it was in my way, and left it behind to walk the rest of the way down the mountain. Just inches to the side, however, I could see the back of the car crushed into the backseat.

I climbed into the driver's seat and rested my hands on the steering wheel. There were a few drops of blood on the top, but when I was sitting in this position, that was the only indication that there was an accident at all. I wrapped my hands around the wheel and leaned my head back against the headrest, closing my eyes. I tried to remember anything. I searched my brain for even the smallest imprint of the sounds, smells, or sights that I might have experienced when the crash happened. Somewhere in the back of my mind I could see the snowflakes falling in front of the windshield and feel the chill from getting into the car and not turning on the heat. I felt a jolt of fear and saw the image of the tree in front of me. My eyes snapped open as I drew in a sharp breath.

"Are you alright?" Micah asked, coming to the still-open driver's side door and leaning down to look at me. "Did you remember something?"

"I'm fine," I said. I let my hands fall away from the steering wheel. "I still don't know what happened. I don't understand how I got here."

I leaned to the side and opened the glove compartment, wondering if there might be anything inside that could tell me more. It was pristine and virtually empty, containing only a slim folder that looked like it had been there since the car was purchased. I snapped the hatch closed and sighed.

"Is there anything I can do?" he asked.

I shook my head.

"Just take me back up to the lodge," I said. "There's no point in me being here."

Micah reached in and offered me his hand. I took it and let him guide me out of the car. He pulled me in to hug me as he closed the door. I clung to him, burying my face in his coat to warm the chill on my skin. When we stepped away from each other, we headed back up the ridge. I struggled with each step and again felt a sense of amazement that he had done this with me in his arms. Though the snow wasn't as deep then, it still would have been difficult, and I squeezed his hand in another thank you.

Nearly an hour later we were sitting in the great room. I was curled up on the couch, my hands wrapped tightly around a hot mug of coffee as I stared into the dancing flames of the fire that Micah had built. This was a real fire, not like the one in the library, and the sound of the logs and smell of the burning wood surrounded me. I drew in a breath of it and felt my lips curl up into a smile as my lungs filled with the smell.

"I love the smell of Rome burning," I said.

Micah straightened and looked at me strangely.

"What?" he asked as he put the fireplace tool back into its stand.

"Spaceship Earth," I said. "Have you ever ridden it? There's a part where the libraries are burning and there's this amazing smell. I know it's supposed to be a little bit scary, but I've always loved the smell. There was a time when Madeline and I thought about starting our own business making handcrafted soaps and candles and that smell was one of the ones that we wanted to try to recreate."

Micah was staring at me, his jaw set.

"Madeline?"

"My sister. The younger one." I took a sip of my coffee and let out a short laugh. "She is going to be so pissed at me when she sees what I did to her car."

The realization of what I had just said, the whole exchange that we had just had, hit me as hard as the impact of the crash and my mouth fell open. I nearly dropped the mug in my hand and Micah took it from me as he came to crouch down in front of me.

"What did you just say?"

I looked at him, feeling almost like I was looking at him for the first time. The familiarity was there in his eyes, but now I knew why. There weren't any questions anymore. Suddenly and painfully, it was all there again.

"I remember. My name is Charlotte Dabney. I came onto the mountain to spend Thanksgiving with my family." I said. I felt my heart clench. "I remember you."

"You do?"

He reached up to touch my face and I pulled away from him.

"We went to high school together. You were on the football team."

You were the gorgeous, popular boy who I was head-over-heels for even before I met Daniel.

Oh, god. Daniel.

I scrambled off the end of the couch and ran toward the memorabilia room. The door was locked, and I pounded on it, letting out my frustration and anger until Micah came up behind me and unlocked it. I ran directly to the high school display in the back corner and pointed at the jersey.

"I went to that high school," I said. "That's why it looked familiar when I first saw it. I couldn't remember, but there was something about it." I reached down and grabbed one of the yearbooks displayed on the lower shelf. I flipped through the pages until I found the senior pictures. "Because we went to school together. You *knew* who I was." I slammed the yearbook down on the surface of a table in front of me and pointed at my picture. "You've known who I was for fucking *years.*"

Micah took a step toward me.

"Charlotte, listen to me."

"No," I said, shaking my head. "No, I don't want to listen to you. How could you do this to me? You must have known who I was as soon as you saw me."

I could see Micah's face from when he was in high school. He was slimmer then, his younger face smooth and bare. The image of him in his football uniform, laughing as he walked through the halls like a king holding court, stood in stark contrast to the rough, bearded man who stood in front of me now. The mountain had changed him. The years had changed him. I knew that they had changed me as well, but not as wholly, not as completely as they had changed Micah. I wondered if even if I had had my memory when I first woke up in the lodge, or if I could remember that first moment when he took me out of the car, if I would have been able to recognize him. I knew that his eyes had stayed with me since high school. The expression of those eyes in the few times that he had looked at me. I never really knew if he was actually looking at me. There were times when we were both going down the hall and he seemed to turn his attention toward me, but he never spoke to me. He never even seemed to acknowledge that I was there. But I always knew that he was there. There was something about him, something that I couldn't explain, that drew me to him even then.

It wasn't just that he was gorgeous. He was beautiful then, in a different way than he was now, in a different way than the other guys I went to school with us. But it wasn't just that that made me want to be near him. Any time I was close to him, or even just looking at him across a room or that one time when I mustered up my courage and went to a football game, I felt somehow changed. I couldn't explain it then, and I couldn't explain it now. In truth, I shouldn't have been afraid of him. We were in the same social circle, were meant to have the same friends. But he was outgoing, loud, boisterous, charismatic. I was shy and quiet, never really able to step into the role that seem to have been made for me. People expected me to be like my sisters. My older sister before me had been the queen of the school. Micah was two years older than me, which meant that if Miranda had been just a year or two younger than she was, it would have been likely that she and Micah would have dated. They would have ruled the halls of the high school without question or opposition. Even those who criticized Micah because he didn't come from the same zip code and wasn't backed by a name that went back decades or even centuries in our town couldn't stand in his way. I was never like that. I didn't like to be the center of attention. I never had the courage or the confidence to even try. I always felt as though I was existing just on the edge of everyone else. I orbited around those who should have been my closest friends and confidants. I orbited around Micah.

"Please, Charlotte," he said. "Just let me explain."

"How are you going to explain this?" I asked angrily. "What could you possibly say that would excuse you for not telling me?"

"I should have told you," he admitted. "I did know who you were as soon as I saw you. At least I thought that I did. It's been a long time since I saw you and I couldn't be completely sure. When I realized that you had lost your memory, I didn't know if I should tell you who I thought that you were. I didn't know if it would cause damage or force you to remember something that you weren't ready to remember yet."

"But you told me my name" I said.

"I did," he said. "I thought that I could at least give you that. I wanted something to call you and the longer that I spent with you, the more confident I was that you were who I thought you were."

"You lied to me. You kept something from me that you had no right to keep from me."

Micah stepped toward me again, but I stepped out of the way. I didn't want him anywhere near me. I wanted to get out of the room and away from him. I was angrier than I could put words to, but I was also hurt beyond description. I couldn't believe that he had done this to me. It felt even more than deceptive and manipulative. It felt abusive. It felt like he was purposely trying to keep my identity and my memories from me so that I wouldn't have any context, so that I wouldn't have any choice as to whether I wanted to stay with him or find a way to leave. He wanted to make sure that he could control me in exactly the same way that I had always been controlled. This was the very thing that I have been trying to escape and I had ended up right back in it.

I maneuvered around Micah and rushed out of the memorabilia room and toward the guest room. I dragged my suitcase out from under the bed where I had tucked it and dropped it down onto the mattress just as I had the day that I had run from my parents' cabin. Some of my clothes were still upstairs in Micah's bedroom, but I didn't care. I had closed the door to the guest room as soon as I stepped in and I didn't intend on opening it again until I had figured out a way that I could get away from the lodge and away from Micah. I didn't want to see him again. Even as I thought this, however, tears burned in my eyes and my heart ached. I had known that my memories were probably going to come back at some point and that it would change things, but I couldn't believe just how quickly and excruciatingly the world around me had crumbled.

After I packed everything that was still in the guest room and the attached bathroom, I zipped the suitcase closed and put it beside the door so that I be able to access it easily. I looked out the window and saw that it had begun to snow again. Behind me the door to the bedroom flew open and I realized that I hadn't locked it. I whipped around and stared at Micah, furious, but also wishing that I could curl into his arms and find the comfort and reassurance that had been there for the last two weeks.

"Go away," I said.

"No," he told me. "Not until you listen to me."

"I don't have to listen to you. I don't have to do anything. That's what got me here in the first place."

"Charlotte, you need to understand my side of this."

"Oh, I understand. You found a helpless woman out in a storm and decided that you would take advantage of the situation."

I hated that I had said the words as soon as I did, and I hated him even more when I saw how they changed Micah's eyes. But the truth was that was exactly how I felt. I had gone from feeling as though he had rescued me to feeling like I had been captured. He hadn't just kept my body. By not telling me my name or what he knew about me, he had kept my mind as well.

"Is that really what you think?" he asked.

All of the tenderness that had built in his voice was now gone. The cold, distant anger that had been there in the first few days had returned.

"What do you want me to think? How else am I supposed to feel? I appreciate that you got me out of that car and brought me here, but what about after that? What happened after I woke up? You could have told me right then what you knew. You could have told me my name, about my family, that we came from the same place. You kept me from being able to find them and to let them know that I'm alright. I can't even imagine how worried they are about me, because of you. They probably think that I'm dead somewhere and don't know where to even look for me because you didn't even have the decency to let me tell them."

"Do you want to know what happened after I found you in that car? Do you really want to know why you're still here?"

"Yes" I said.

I was shaking, and I was fighting the tears that were still stinging in my eyes. He didn't deserve them. I had cried far too many tears for Daniel and all of the pain that he had caused me, and I knew that if I was honest with myself, I would admit that I had cried tears in high school for Micah as well. I had cried enough. I had given enough of myself. I was done.

"I did know who you were," he said. "I tried to tell myself that I might be wrong, but I knew that I wasn't. I would remember your face no matter what. But I didn't know who you were when I first saw the car. All I knew was that someone had crashed into a tree and there was a storm coming and they were in danger. I've lived up on this mountain by myself for years and I know the danger. I have learned to protect myself and to be sure that I was ready for whatever came. I knew that whoever might be in that car didn't have that knowledge. If they did, they wouldn't be on that road. That is an access road that is only used to get this far up in the mountain and my lodge is the only thing this far up on the mountain. Whoever was driving that car was obviously lost and hadn't paid attention to any of the warnings that had told them to stop driving and find shelter. I went to the car to find and help whoever was in the car. Finding you wasn't in my plans."

"And when you did? When you did realize that it was me, what changed?"

"Only how strongly I felt about making sure that you were safe. I didn't know why you would be up here, but I could see that you were hurt and then you passed out in my arms. I had no choice but to bring you up here and do my best to take care of you. That meant bringing you into the guest room and cleaning the cut on your head. It meant making sure that Scout stayed with you. It also meant that as soon as I knew that you were sleeping peacefully, I went and called the rangers. I couldn't get through, but I kept trying. I kept the radio on and listened for any missing persons announcement. There weren't any."

"What do you mean?" I asked.

"There weren't any missing persons announcements," he repeated. "Nothing came over the radio. There were no indications that anyone had reported a single person missing on this mountain. They still haven't. I finally got through to emergency Personnel, but they also hadn't heard anything about a missing person or a missing vehicle. Because of that, they wouldn't put any more priority on getting up here than they already had. They needed to take care of things that had happened lower on the mountain and help the people in the valley. They said that they would keep an ear out for anyone saying that a woman had disappeared while traveling on the mountain or that they were looking for a lost vehicle, and that they would call me as soon as they heard. I haven't heard back from them. I tried. I tried to make sure that your family knew that you were safe and that we could find a way to get you back to them, but there was nothing else that I could do. They weren't looking for you, Charlotte. They aren't looking for you."

"You're lying," I said, fighting to control my emotions.

"There would be no reason for me to lie," Micah said. "If there were people looking for you and they found out that you had been here, don't you think that would be a problem? I don't just remember you. I remember your family, too. I know how they feel about their money and their power. And I know how they feel about the people they don't think should have either. If they have been trying to find you, they would have been able to demand and pay and force their way to the top of the priority list. And they would make sure that anyone who had anything to do with you missing paid for it. I kept you here to protect you. I didn't tell you who you are or what I know about you or your life because I didn't know if you would want to remember. I didn't know if you would want to know."

I glared at Micah. I was seething. My heart was pounding so hard in my chest I felt like it would crack through my ribs or come up through my throat. I gritted my teeth to give more strength to my voice.

"Get out."

Micah turned and walked out of the room, not bothering to close the door behind him. I waited until I heard the stomping of his footsteps going up the stairs toward his bedroom. And then I did the only thing that I knew. The only thing that I could think of when the world was crashing down around me, and I didn't know the next step that I should take.

I ran.

Chapter Twelve

Micah

I should have told her. I should have fucking told her.

No, I should have insisted that the police come and get her.

I should have brought her down the mountain myself and left her at the nearest ranger station.

There was an intensity of anger in me that I didn't know was possible. I had been angry before. I had been infuriated before. But I never felt anything like this. The anger that I was feeling was only a thin cover for the pain that was deeper inside of me. Even as I tried to convince myself that I shouldn't have done what I had for Charlotte, that I should have gotten her off of my hands as soon as I could, I knew that that wasn't practical. It wasn't reality. I had been telling the truth when I told her that I went down to the car when I saw it smashed against the tree because I was worried about anybody who might be inside. But I had also been telling the truth when I told her that the instant I saw her face, I was far more worried and knew that I would do anything that I needed to do to protect her. That meant protecting her from the snow and from the possible effects of her injuries, but it also meant protecting her from herself and from the world around her.

I did remember her family. I remembered them as arrogant and pretentious. I had never interacted with either of her sisters, but I had heard from a few guys who had just how miserable it was to try to get in with their parents. It wasn't that they were protective of their daughters. They weren't trying to guard their hearts or defend their honor. Instead, they were trying to craft and defend their own reputation. They looked down on anyone who didn't have money and whose name didn't appear on at least one building downtown. It didn't matter who you were as a person or what you had accomplished. All that mattered was who had bred you. Even if I had tried to approach Charlotte during those high school years, it would have been futile. Even if I had been able to get beyond the judgement and expectations of my friends and the people who acted like my friends but who never actually were. I never would have been able to be close to her. Her parents never would have accepted a boy from the wrong side of the tracks. We didn't have a name that anybody would recognize. We didn't have money. What we did have was secrets. And those were enough to keep me well outside of the realm of any man who the Dabneys would consider acceptable for one of their daughters. I couldn't give them a good reputation. I couldn't give them higher social standing. I couldn't give them more power or more money. That was nothing that I could offer them, so they didn't care what I might be able to offer Charlotte.

They really weren't all that different from my family. The only difference was a couple of generations and a tremendous amount of luck. Of course, that didn't matter to them. In their eyes, they were as important and privileged as any of the founding families of the country, and they were loathed to even acknowledge those who might not agree with them. They didn't hear the whispers. They didn't hear the people who knew exactly where they had come from and who they still were, or the rumors that were still spread about them by those who weren't impressed by the newness of their success and prevalence. If they did hear it, they didn't acknowledge it.

I paced through my bedroom until I felt like I calmed down enough to talk to her again. I hated the way that she had looked at me when she accused me of taking advantage of her. I didn't want her to think that I would ever do anything to hurt her, especially knowing the hurt that she had already suffered. I didn't know the full extent of what she had gone through, but I knew that it was enough to have shaped the way that she looked at me. I headed back down the stairs and found Scout circling in the great room. He was whimpering, his tail pointing straight out the way that it did when he wanted to chase something.

"I can't play with you right now," I told him.

He circled a few more times and then ran for the door. He looked back, noticing that I wasn't following him, and ran toward me again.

"I can't play with you right now," I said again. "I need to go talk to Charlotte."

I made my way through the house and toward the guest bedroom. I expected to find the door closed again and intended to knock on it this time, but instead the door was standing open. I looked inside and found the room empty. My heart immediately sank. I turned and looked at Scout who was standing in the hall behind me looking at me as if to suggest that he knew something I didn't. I walked out into the lodge and began to run from room to room, calling for her. I checked the library, but the chair where she sat to read beside the fireplace was empty. I looked in each of the bathrooms. I checked the living room. I even went to the memorabilia room, thinking that maybe I had left the door unlocked and she was in there again going through the mementos from high school. The house was empty and quiet. She was gone.

I looked at Scout.

"Where is she, boy? Where did she go?"

He wagged his tail and I immediately went to the mudroom to put on my layers of heavy clothes. She had gone out into the snow and I knew by the trek that we had made to the car that she wasn't prepared to be in the woods by herself, particularly as the afternoon grew later. As soon as I zipped up my coat, I burst out into the snow. The light snowfall that had begun earlier was still only letting a soft, gentle amount of snow drift down and I was thankful at least for that. But the cold was incredibly bitter as the wind picked up around me. I worried that she was going to have very little time. I looked around at the snow, trying to find her tracks so that I could follow them. I could see our footsteps from earlier and I wondered if she might have followed them. I started into the woods, moving as quickly as I could through the deep snow. I pulled my scarf up over my mouth and nose, so that I could breathe the warm air rather than filling my lungs with a sharp chill. This helped me to move faster and I kept my head moving back and forth so I could scan as much of the trees and expanse of snow as I possibly could. My voice was muffled by the scarf, and occasionally I took it away so that I could scream her name. My voice echoed back to me, as if reminding me how alone I was on the mountain.

Fear had started to fill me as soon as I realized that she had left the house and it was only intensifying with every step that I took. I had hoped that she would follow the path of our footsteps directly back down the road, not into the woods when I noticed her footsteps veering away from our tracks. I couldn't understand why she would have turned away from the path or where she could think that she was going, and the worry spiked up even higher. I step to the side so that I wouldn't obliterate her footsteps and begin to follow them. Scout followed my lead and began to tromp through the snow to my side. It was so deep that there were times when he sank down to his neck and I had to pause to dig him back out. Each time this happened I felt like more and more time was slipping away. I was desperate. I had to find her.

I continued on, moving as fast as I could and screaming her name with every breath that I pulled in. The sun was beginning to set, and the light was getting dusky around me. Finally, several yards in front of me, I saw a shape in the snow. I ran toward it and dropped to my knees at Charlotte's side. She was lying on the ground, curled onto one hip with her face up towards the sky. I tucked one hand under her head and lifted it.

"Charlotte," I said. "Charlotte, open your eyes."

Her eyes fluttered, but didn't open. She was only wearing a sweatshirt over a long-sleeved shirt and I realized that she had left her coat in my bedroom. I couldn't believe that she would do something so stupid as to go out in this weather without the layers that she needed, and the guilt clamped down on me like a vice. I knew that I hadn't handled the confrontation the way that I should have. I shouldn't have been so aggressive with her. I shouldn't have walked away from her. I gently laid her back down into the snow and stood, unzipping my coat. I took off my layers down to the thermal shirt that I wore closest to my skin and wrapped them around her. I scooped her up into my arms and cradled her close to my chest as I started back toward the house. I knew that the temperature around me was bitter and that exposing my skin this way was dangerous, but I didn't care. All that mattered was getting Charlotte safe again.

It at once felt like the walk back to the lodge took hours and was over in moments. I stomped my feet on the mat to shake off the snow and ran into the great room to lay Charlotte out on the rug in front of the fire. She was moaning softly, and her eyelids lifted slowly to look at me.

"Micah," she whispered.

"Shhhhh," I soothed her. "It's alright. I'm here. You're safe now." I drew in a breath. "You're home."

I peeled away all of her wet clothes and wrapped her body in blankets. She was shaking, but soon her body calmed. I wrapped my arms around her and kissed her cheek, wanting the reassurance of the feeling of her skin as much as I wanted to reassure her. I wanted her to know that it didn't matter anymore. Nothing mattered anymore but the fact that she was here with me and that I was determined not to let anything happen to her again.

****

Charlotte

The next day I finally felt like myself again. Micah and I hadn't talked about what had happened yet. He had been giving me the space and the quiet that I needed to process everything, and I was trying to put myself back into a normal rhythm of life. I missed him and as if that was enough to draw him to me, I heard him coming up the stairs as I was making the bed. I was finishing piling the comforter up when Micah walked into the bedroom. Without a word, he crossed the room to me and took me by the hips. He captured my mouth and held me close, sucking on my bottom lip. Micah guided me back and tipped me onto the mattress, positioning me so that I lay with my head on the pillow. I was wearing only thin lounge pants and a shirt, and Micah peeled away the shirt, tossing it aside unceremoniously. He ran his palm down the center of my chest before dipping his head down to indulge a craving with a long lick across my skin.

I lifted my head and reciprocated the gesture across his bare shoulder. I tasted the primal, salty flavor of sweat and I ran my tongue along his skin. My hands slid up to his waist and I could feel ribs beneath his smooth skin as he murmured in response to the lick. When he was carrying me back through the snow his shirt had lifted, exposing some of his skin to the elements, giving it a hint of color. The subtle contrast between this slightly reddened skin and the skin that had been protected by clothing was unexpectedly arousing. It was as if that skin was emerging solely for the purpose of luring me to it to worship it with my fingertips, my tongue, and my own vulnerable skin.

Micah continued his trail of kisses up my body, occasionally lifting his head to blow a stream of cool air against the dampened trail of skin. I gripped the covers beside me to control myself, enjoying every moment of the attention that he was giving me, but also the luscious way his body was responding to the touch of my mouth and my hands, and the taste of my skin against his lips. I wanted this to last as long as it could, but I also wanted Micah to let go of the control that he was showing. I wanted him to give in to the desire that we were both feeling. I needed him. I needed the connection, the validation of his touch as much as the release of energy, frustration, and pent-up emotion that I was feeling.

As if my very thoughts had urged and compelled him, Micah suddenly lifted up so that his body pinned me down. I could feel the intoxicating pressure of his already hardening erection pressing into my lower belly and Micah stare down at me with fire in his eyes. He licked his lips with anticipation and touched his hand behind my head to pull our mouths together. I complied with the guidance, pressing my hands to his back so that he would stretch across me more fully. The warmth of his chest pressing down on to my own and our mouths playing across each other sent my arousal surging further, and I tightened my grasp around Micah to deepen our kiss. I didn't want to lose the taste of his mouth yet.

Micah's lips parted, and his tongue sought mine. I welcomed it into my mouth, greeting it with my own so that they tangled and explored with greater familiarity. The thought of how close we had come to losing each other and the knowledge that I was now offering myself to him with full understanding, full awareness of who I was and why I was here, made the kiss even more desperate. I nipped at Micah's bottom lip and he pulled back to stare into my eyes. I reached between us and started to push the waistband of Micah's pants down.

"I was worried you wouldn't come for me," I said.

"I will always come for you."

With those words, Micah positioned himself on his knees between my legs and shucked his pants. He then brought his mouth down to my waistband, running his mouth along the center of my chest and belly as he went. He let the tip of his tongue slip beneath my waistband and ran it back and forth between my hip bones. I whimpered and lifted my hips, inviting him to undress me the rest of the way. He did, slipping them off and letting them fall off the side of the bed, onto the floor. Filled with a sudden compulsion, I pressed my hands to Micah's chest and rolled him so that he was on his back and I was sprawled on top of him. I kissed my way down his body, relishing the feeling of his muscles and the smell of his body. I gripped his hip with one hand and the base of his cock with the other. Micah cried out as I ran my tongue up the underside of his cock to the head. When the progress of my tongue reached the tip, I grasped his shaft harder and used the tip of my tongue along the edge of the head. I completed the outline, taking a few seconds to focus my attention on the bundle of nerves just beneath the tip, then licked the slit, letting the tip of my tongue dip inside slightly. Micah's legs were beginning to shake, but he made no move to stop me.

I opened my mouth and took Micah's cock inside. He groaned, and I felt need rush through my body at the breathtaking sensation of my tongue swirling around his erection. I sucked deeply to draw his cock closer to my throat. Micah buried his hand into my hair with one hand as I felt the other grip my shoulder. He lifted his hips to thrust into my mouth with each suck. I knew that he wasn't going to be able to hold out much longer. I had learned the signs of his body and the pitch of the sounds that poured out of him as he lost himself in the ecstasy that we created together. Finally, Micah's head arched back with a deep, animal yell as I felt the pressure in his cock peak and then become a series of fast pulses. Micah gasped for air as I cleaned his cock with my lips and tongue, savoring the taste of him, filling my heart and body with him.

Micah was still shuddering and struggling to draw in even breaths when I propped myself up on my elbow beside him and gazed into his face. He rested his hand into the center of my chest and paused, feeling my heartbeat, before guiding me onto my back. He straddled me on his knees and touched his mouth to the underside of my jaw. He moved slowly, but his gradual pace didn't feel timid. Instead, there was a fierce strength behind his movements as if he wanted to display his dominance by ensuring that I fully felt and experienced every purposeful touch and breath.

His mouth made its way to one breast and he cupped it, lifting it so that he could trace the edge of my nipple with his tongue. He opened his mouth and took my breast into it, suckling me as he kneaded my other breast with his palm. When the breast in his mouth was heavy and hot, my nipple hardened, he withdrew it from his mouth and repeated the attention on the other. The backs of his fingers touched my belly between us and ran down it with a feathery touch until he reached his cock. He flattened his hand on the top of his shaft to press his erection to my belly and rocked his hips, so I could feel it run along my heated skin.

Droplets of slick fluid were slipping from the tip of his cock, making it glide along my belly and bringing a strong ache between my thighs. His mouth ran up my chest and to my ear. I felt his teeth nip playfully at my skin.

"Roll over," he whispered into my ear.

I moaned at the eroticism in his voice and rolled onto my belly. Micah's hand slipped under my stomach and lifted it until I was positioned on my hands and knees. I felt Micah lean forward to stretch over me and his tongue touched my spine between my shoulder blades. It ran down my spine, making me tremble. Suddenly his knee pushed between mine, easing my legs apart. Micah's hands cupped my ass, squeezing deeply into the muscles. He drew his hands apart, exposing me to more intimate attention. I felt vulnerable, but also intensely turned on and I pushed back toward him. I gasped at the feeling of Micah's hot breath against my dripping opening and then my throbbing clit, a sensation that made my toes curl and my stomach clench. The tip of Micah's tongue touched my skin and my back arched, my head dropping back as I let out a strangled cry in response to the explosive feeling. He had licked me before, but being in this position and having his mouth capturing me from behind was new and nearly overwhelming. Micah pushed further, his tongue exploring me deeply and without hesitation. His touch coaxed me to relax and open to him, and I felt myself relinquishing to him. I reached around to stroke Micah's cock, encouraging it to harden even more.

I felt moments from a mind-blowing orgasm when Micah's mouth and hand left my body. I had only a few seconds to catch my breath and let myself cool before I heard the sound of a condom packet opening and then felt him behind me again. His hand gripped my shoulder and applied pressure as if to pull me backwards toward him. I felt the tip of his erection touch my opening and I pressed back into it, craving having him inside me again.

"Do you want me?" Micah asked.

My breath caught in my throat and I pushed back harder.

"Yes," I groaned.

Micah tightened his grip on my shoulder and hip and pressed forward to meet my seeking pressure. His engorged cock slipped inside me and eased deeper with each breath. The sensation fulfilled me and soon I felt myself giving into Micah completely. He brought his hand between my thighs and massaged into my clit as he started to pump into me. With each roll of his hips I knew that there was so much more than just my body that I was relinquishing to Micah as each day passed. I was offering my body, my heart, and my soul to him.

The movement of his hips caused Micah's hand to stroke my peak with the same rhythm as his thrusts inside me and I felt myself nearly overwhelmed by the layers of sensation that flowed over me. Within seconds I felt my body starting to tense. The deep, grunting sounds coming from Micah told me that he was on the same rushing path toward orgasm. The thought that we were fully in sync, entrenched in the blissful experience together, drove me toward the brink even faster. I opened my eyes to look down and watch Micah's hand bringing on the waves of a powerful climax. Micah cried out and I felt him thrust as deep within me as he could. He held himself in place as he pulsed frantically, satisfying me completely.

After a few moments, Micah withdrew and we both collapsed down onto the bed. He reached down and pulled the covers up so that we could slip under them, holding his arms open so that I could get under with him and tuck up against the side of his body. I kissed him and then curled onto my side so that Micah could wrap around me, holding me close so that he could kiss along the back of my shoulder. His slow, even breathing made his chest and stomach press against my back, further tightening our connection with each inhale. I nuzzled back into him, wanting his warmth and to touch every inch of him that I could. I never wanted to leave this spot.

Chapter Thirteen

Micah

"I was trying to get away from Daniel."

Charlotte's voice was so low that I wasn't even sure that I had heard her. She was curled on her side and I was curled behind her, my body molded to hers as my hand ran along her stomach. I had thought that she was asleep and was starting to drift away myself when her words woke me back up.

"What?" I asked.

"That's why I crashed into the tree. I was trying to get away from Daniel."

She rolled over and slid slightly closer so that our faces were just a few inches from each other.

"Who's Daniel?" I asked.

"He used to be my boyfriend," she said.

I had an immediate reaction to the word, my jaw tightening and my stomach burning angrily. Though I obviously knew that she had been in a relationship before, hearing her talk about it was more difficult than I expected it to be.

"How long were you together?" I asked.

She looked at me with slightly narrowed eyes as if she couldn't understand why I would ask the question.

"Since high school," she said.

The revelation hit me in the center of the chest and the image of the guy in the hallway with Charlotte snapped into my mind again. I saw the way that she was looking at him, the sheer terror in her eyes. There wasn't any hesitation behind the fear, no questions or surprise. She knew that this was going to happen. It had likely happened to her countless times before. I knew that expression all too well. I had seen it in my mother's eyes. I knew I had had it in my own.

"You're still with him?" I asked.

"I was," she admitted.

I sat up, staring down at her.

"How could you still be with him? I saw the way that he treated you."

Her eyes widened, and I knew that this was too much. She was finally opening up to me and I needed to give her the chance to do it. As much as I didn't want to think that anything had hurt her or that she had ever gone through anything worse than what I had seen in that hallway, I wanted to know what had happened so that I knew for certain that I would never let it happen again. I settled back down and eased closer to her so that our thighs touched, and our feet tangled.

"I know how he treated me," she said. "I also remember that you protected me. I never forgot that. Thank you."

"If you never forgot it, why did you stay with him? I had to physically tear him away from you. Why didn't you just leave him right then?"

"I tried to," she said. "I tried to leave him. I told him that I couldn't take it anymore, that I didn't want to be with him anymore because of the way that he treated me and that it wasn't what I wanted."

"But?"

She let out an exasperated sound.

"You saw me in high school, Micah. You know how I was."

"You were beautiful."

"No, I wasn't."

"Yes, you were. You were captivating."

"If I was so captivating, why did you never talk to me? I was right there all the time. We were in the same hallway every day. I even went to one of your football games. You never even spoke a word to me."

"You did go to that game to see me."

"Of course, I did. You didn't even know that I was there."

"Yes, I did," I said, nodded. A smile was curving my lips despite the sadness in her voice. Just knowing that I hadn't been wrong, that she had been there for me as much as I felt like she had lifted my heart. "I knew that you were there. I saw you sitting there in the stands. You were all alone."

She nodded.

"The few people I had who would consider themselves my friends weren't exactly the football game type."

"I'm sorry that I didn't talk to you."

"Why didn't you?"

I didn't know what to say. I didn't know how to explain to her what it had been like for me when I was in high school, before I had learned not to care about what anyone thought of me. It made me feel weak. It made me feel like I had somehow failed her even before I knew her.

"I wanted to. Every time that I saw you, I thought about talking to you."

"I wish you had."

"I wish I had, too. Maybe things would have been different."

She shook her head.

"It wasn't your job to save me then, Micah. I should have been stronger and more confident. That was the problem that I had. I had absolutely no confidence. I wasn't like my sisters. I didn't take to people. I didn't feel pretty. I wasn't particularly talented at anything like they were. There was just always a way that I felt like I was a few steps behind them. I shouldn't have let it get to me, but I did. It totally took away my confidence and my security in myself, and my parents pushing me to be the perfect daughter and find the perfect match didn't help. It was all working against me. Of course, I didn't see it at the time."

"Then you met Daniel."

She sighed.

"Then I met Daniel. Well, then I started dating Daniel. I had known him basically my entire life. We grew up together. That's why our parents thought it was so perfect when we started dating. They could already see the number signs and the business-growing wedding announcement. I was just so happy that someone was paying attention to me. He seemed like he actually recognized that I was there, that I was a person. Does that make sense? It seemed like everyone else sort of looked through me. They knew that I existed, but it didn't really have much consequence."

"I understand," I said.

I really felt like I did, if from the opposite angle. I was just like her, but on the other side of the spectrum. People knew that I existed, and I was of far too much consequence for all of them. Everything that I did and said meant far too much when it shouldn't have. She felt like people saw through her because she wasn't able to live up to what she thought that they expected her to be. I felt like people saw through me because they only saw what they had crafted of me and what I had crafted of myself. None really knew me or what was behind the uniform. None of them really cared.

"Was he always like that to you?"

"No," she said. "He was actually really wonderful in the beginning. He was so sweet and attentive. He made me feel beautiful and like I was the most interesting person he had ever met. Everything that I said to him, he hung on. Every suggestion that I made, he made it seem like it was the most brilliant thing that he had ever heard. It drew me in and I was enraptured with him. I didn't see what was really happening. I had no idea that all he was doing was manipulating me. He was gaining control of me so that I would become dependent on him without even realizing it. The change was so gradual that by the time he became aggressive and abusive, I felt like that must have been the way that it always was and that if it wasn't, that I had done something to deserve it."

I reached forward and stroked her cheek with my thumb.

"There is nothing that you did that made you deserve the way that he treated you. No more than my mother deserved the way that my father treated her, or I deserved the way that he treated me. What he did was his fault and something that was wrong with him. Not you."

"Micah," she murmured softly. "I'm so sorry. I didn't know."

"No one did," I admitted. "It's not exactly something that we wanted to talk about much."

"What happened to him?"

"Prison," he said. "He died there. Apparently, the convicts he was housed with weren't too fond of him once they learned what he had done to his wife and son."

She didn't flinch. Instead, she nodded, understanding in her eyes.

"Good."

I wanted to move on. I just wanted the conversation to shift away from me and back to her.

"Tell me more. Tell me what happened."

"I tried to get away from him," she said, bringing the conversation all the way back. "But he came back pleading, pretending to be remorseful. He acted like I had hurt him so much and he had finally realized what he was doing. He came up with every excuse that he possibly could and begged me to give him another chance."

"What did your parents think? They had to have known the way that he was treating you."

"They didn't," she said. "They adore Daniel. They did from the first day that we were together, and they still do now. They think that he's wonderful, but beyond that, they see just how valuable he could be to them. He's from an extremely wealthy, influential family, and there's nothing that my parents love more than money and influence. I tried a few times to tell them, but they were just so hopeful, I didn't want to disappoint them. I wanted them to be happy and to be proud of me."

"So, you went back to him."

She nodded.

"Again and again and again. For the rest of high school."

"I wish I had known."

"You didn't even talk to me after you punched him. You just walked away."

"I didn't want to make things worse for you. I knew that if I stayed there, there would be a brawl, and I didn't want you to have to see that. I figured that you had been through enough and hoped that if I just walked away, that you would do the same. I wanted to find you after that, but I graduated."

"Life happened."

I nodded.

"Life happened."

She let out a breath again.

"We stayed together through high school and into college. There were times when it seemed like he had grown out of that behavior and that things were actually going to be good, but every time that that happened, it just got worse again. That's when I started to learn more about myself. I discovered the things that I was actually interested in and that I was good at. I realized that I wasn't like my sisters, but that that was alright. They were fantastic at being them, but I was going to learn to be as good at being me as I possibly could."

"How did Daniel feel about that?"

"About as good as you probably think that he did. It took so much longer than it ever should have. I look back now, and I don't understand how I couldn't have seen what he was doing. The more that he saw me learning and growing, the harsher that he became. Every little bit that I progressed, he dragged me back. The worst part about it was that I wanted so much for it to work. I wanted to believe that I hadn't wasted all of those years. I thought that maybe if he could see how much I was improving myself and that I was enjoying life so much more now that I was feeling more confident and aware of myself, that somehow, he would change, too. I really believed that we would end up having the life that we had always dreamed of having."

"Did you really dream of having a life with him?"

"I thought that I did. I had been told for so long that that was what I wanted, that I believed it. It wasn't until about a year ago that it really sank in that it wasn't what I wanted. It took months, dark, brutal months, for me to finally tear myself away from him for good."

"But you said that you were running from him when you crashed into the tree."

"My parents rented a cabin up here for Thanksgiving to spend time with the three of us, my sisters' husbands, and my two nieces. They are both pregnant and it was turning into an actually pretty perfect family holiday when they got over chastising me for not being married or pregnant."

"What happened?"

"Apparently Daniel never really accepted that things are over between us. Because I wouldn't listen to him anymore, though, he went over my head to my parents. He told them how worried he was about me and that my time in college had really changed me. He implied that I was on some sort of dark, self-destructive path and that he just wanted to save me. So, they invited him to the cabin."

"Without telling you?" I asked.

"Apparently they thought it would be an amazing surprise. They just couldn't understand why I was so upset when I saw him. He made it very clear that he expected me to come right back to him like I always had, but I told him that I wasn't. That's when I ran."

"What did he do to you, Charlotte?"

She looked at me and for the first time that evening I saw a flicker of fear in her eyes. It was as if she didn't want to give me all of the details, like she didn't want to admit what she had actually gone through because she was afraid of what I would think of her. Finally, she licked her lips, looked down at the mattress for a second as if to reassure and anchor herself, and then begin to describe the years that she had spent with Daniel.

I couldn't believe what she was telling me. I was more and more horrified with each detail that she gave me. I had hoped for so many years that she had gotten away from that guy. I hoped that seeing someone protect her would show her that she mattered and give her some sort of boost to find a way out of the situation. Knowing that she hadn't brought a painful blend of emotions to my mind into my heart. I was saddened and disappointed, but I also felt pity and even anger. But I felt those things as much for myself as I did for Charlotte. Listening to her brought back all the memories from my childhood and everything that I had gone through with my father, and everything that I had seen my mother suffer and endure at his hands. I felt like Charlotte had been following the same horrible path my mother had. I wondered in that moment if this was inevitable for some people. I wondered if it could be that it was just part of life. Just that thought alone was sickening. I had done everything that I could for my mother and now I would do everything that I could for Charlotte. I wouldn't let her suffer that fate.

"I'm sorry that you had to go through any of that," I said when Charlotte finished. "I know how it feels to be mistreated. It's unfair and there's nothing that you could have done to deserve it."

"It's different for you, though," she said.

"What do you mean?" I asked.

"It was your father. You didn't have a choice. You didn't get to choose who your father was or the fact that he lived in the house with you. There was nothing that you could do. You were a child and you are at his mercy. I chose the path that I took. I chose Daniel. I chose to listen to him. I chose to let him treat me the way that he did. And I chose to stay."

I shook my head.

"It isn't your fault, Charlotte. Nothing that he did is your fault. And you're right, I didn't have a choice about the way that my father treated me. But I do know what it's like to be mistreated by someone who you're supposed to love, and think that you might have a future with."

"What do you mean? " she asked.

I hadn't intended to talk to her about this. I didn't want to tell her. I didn't even want to say the name or go back and experience those emotions again. But I felt like I needed to share this with her. I wanted her to know everything about me.

"The crash with a drunk driver didn't just end my football career, I told her. I was engaged when I was in college. Her name was Helen and she was in the same type of social circle as Daniel. Privilege and conceit all the way. But of course, I didn't see that. I just saw the pretty girl who liked my attention and looked good on my arm. I saw the doors that opened up for me because I was with her. I really did believe that we had a future together. But when I got hurt and wasn't able to play like I used to, things changed. The harder I worked to recover and to rehabilitate, the more time that she was spending away from me. Instead of being there beside me and supporting me as I went through this, she was becoming more and more distant. Then I found out that I would never be able to play again. I hoped that she would be there for me. She felt like the only thing that I had left. Then I found out that she had been sleeping with my best friend. In an instant, she was gone too.

Everything I thought. Everything I believe. It was all gone. I didn't have a future anymore. I barely even knew who I was."

"I'm so sorry," she said. She leaned forward then kissed me. "I know who you are."

I kissed her back and felt her ease a little closer to me. She suddenly looked exhausted, as if the conversation had completely drained her. Her eyes fluttered closed and within seconds she had fallen asleep. I felt an even stronger compulsion to protect her now. Night had always been the worst time with my father and even though I knew the dangers that both of us had face were over now, I couldn't bear the thought of anything else happening to her, even if it was just having to be afraid.

Chapter Fourteen

Charlotte

I was sitting in the great room curled up in the corner of the couch when Micah came back inside the next morning. He had been out checking the smoke houses and on a whim, I had picked up my cell phone. I realized that I hadn't touched it since the first night that I was there in the lodge with him. It was the longest that I had gone without using my phone since I had gotten it, and it was an amazing revelation that I had not only been able to get by without it, that I had actually enjoyed not feeling so accessible to everyone. The battery had long since died and I dug through my bag to find the extra charger that I always kept packed. I plugged it in without thinking about its connectivity and was surprised when it turned on and showed that my service has been restored. Now I was sitting with it in my hands, staring down at the screen, trying to decide what to do. I glanced up and saw Micah looking at me questioningly.

"Is something wrong?" he asked.

I shook my head.

"No. At least I don't think so. I don't really know. I'm not sure what I'm supposed to do."

"What do you mean?"

"My phone has service again. I'm trying to decide if I should call my parents."

"That's up to you," he said.

There was a slight gruffness in his voice and I knew that he was worried about me.

I looked up at him.

"When was the last time that you listened to the radio? When was the last time that you talked to the rangers and found out if anyone have been reported missing?"

"It's been a few days," he admitted.

"So, it's entirely possible that they're looking for me now," I said. "Maybe they have been all along and were just going through different channels. At least I could let them know that I'm alright."

Despite what Micah had told me about my parents not reporting me or Madeline's car missing, I still couldn't wrap my head around the thought that they weren't even wondering what had happened to me. I'd been gone for two weeks. My phone registered several missed calls, but no voicemails and no text messages. They had to be looking for me. Maybe they had even put together a search party. I began to feel somewhat guilty, a feeling that I was not on accustomed to when it came to how my parents viewed my behavior. I felt bad for the people that were trudging through the snow looking for me, wondering if I was alive, when I had been here in the lodge blissfully happy, safe, and warm.

"I think I have to call them," I said. "They're probably worried about me and don't even know what to do. I'll just let them know that I'm fine and that'll be it."

Micah didn't argue with me. He walked out of the room and into the kitchen as I scrolled through my contacts until I found my mother's phone number. It rang several times before she picked it up.

"I was wondering when you would finally get around to calling."

No hello. No I was worried about you. Nothing.

"Hello to you, too, mother."

"So, to what do I owe the great honor of you finally getting in touch with me? Have you decided that it's time to apologize?"

I was stunned at the statement.

"Apologize? You expect me to apologize?"

"Of course, I do. I can't believe how you behaved. Do you have any idea how uncomfortable you made the rest of the family, or how much you upset Daniel?"

"You're seriously still stuck on Daniel?" I asked, my voice creeping up louder and more intense. "Haven't you even wondered where I was for the last two weeks?"

"No," my mother said. "It's not like you haven't just stormed off in a tizzy before. All of us just assumed that you were having a temper tantrum and that eventually you would get over it and come back. There's really no point in any of us trying to reason with you when you're acting like that."

"Acting like what exactly, Mom?"

"You know exactly what I mean. You just stomped out of the cabin, stole your sister's car, and drove off into the night without even a word."

"I didn't steal Madeline's car. If you hadn't noticed, she didn't even report it missing. Of course, you didn't report me missing either."

"You weren't missing. You are having a fit and you decided to go off and be by yourself. What point exactly did you think that you were making? What did you think that you were going to accomplish by behaving that way? Daniel had already come all the way out there just for you."

"He didn't come out there for me," I scoffed. "He came out there for you. He came out there to impress you and try to convince you of what a wonderful person he was because he doesn't want you to know who he really is."

"Don't start that again, Charlotte. Don't make up more things about him just because it makes you feel better about yourself and the way that you acted while you were in school. He told us all about it, and frankly I am mortified that you would behave that way. Not just for us, but for Daniel. You should have seen how devastated he was when he was talking about you. He is so incredibly worried about you and wants nothing more than what's best for you. You are luckier than you could possibly imagine to have a man like that love you. You certainly don't deserve it. And you completely ruined Thanksgiving for all of us."

I couldn't even believe what I was hearing. My mother had always been judgmental and put herself before everybody else, being fully willing to ignore things that were inconvenient or unpleasant if she thought that they could benefit her in some way. But she had never been so cold. I wondered what Daniel could have possibly told her that had contorted her view of me so much.

"I'll have you know that you are absolutely right," I said. "I am luckier than I could possibly imagine to be loved so much by a man like the one who loves me. But it's not Daniel. It has never been Daniel. Daniel loves nothing and no one but himself. The man I love is the one who's been taking care of me for the last two weeks. He's the one who rescued me when I drove through the storm and crashed Madeline's car into a tree. He saved my life."

My mother let out a sigh that sounded as though she were listening to a teenage girl throw a fit because her daddy didn't buy her the right color car.

"Don't be so dramatic, Charlotte. I don't know where you've been or what you've been doing, but all of us have had enough. We've already left the cabin and gone home, and we expect to see you tomorrow. Goodbye."

I let out an infuriated growl and threw my phone across the couch. I curled my knees up to my chest and buried my face in them.

The touch of Micah's hand on my back made me jump and I turned around to look at him. I realized with a knot in my stomach that he had been standing there during my conversation.

"How much did you hear?" I asked.

"Enough," he said.

"Look, about what I said. About..."

"About spending the last two weeks with a man who loves you?"

I felt heat burning across my cheeks and wanted to curl up and disappear.

"My mother was talking about Daniel and saying how lucky I was to have a man like him love me," I said. "I just said that to try to..."

"It doesn't matter," he said. My heart sank, but then he walked around in front of the couch and crouched down to look at me. "It doesn't matter why you said it. It's true."

"It is?" I asked breathlessly.

"Yes," Micah said. "I love you, Charlotte. I have for so long, but it's only since seeing each other again that I really let myself feel it. I might not come from the best family and there might be a lot of things in my past that I'm not proud of, but what I can tell you is that I love you with every fiber of my being and with every beat of my heart. I love you more than my next breath and there is nothing that you could ever do or that could ever happen that would change that or that would make me let you get hurt."

My breath was caught in my throat and tears stung in my eyes.

"Micah," I started.

He reached out and took both of my hands in his. He brought them up to his mouth and kissed them then brought them to his chest and pressed them to his heart.

"You said that you spent two weeks with the man you love."

"I did," I said. "And I meant it. I love you, Micah. I don't care what kind of family you come from. I don't care what your last name is or what you've gone through. I don't care about anything in your past except for me. You have always been there. Even when neither of us realized it. You protected me, and even though I couldn't protect myself, I never forgot that. That was a moment that was more precious to me then I could ever tell you because it was a moment when I realized that I could be worth more than what Daniel told me I was. I don't know what I did to deserve it, and there's probably nothing that I could have done to deserve it, but you have rescued me again and again. But that's not the only reason that I love you. I love you because of who you are, who you have always been, and who you will be. And I can only hope that I will know that man, too."

"I want you to know every bit of me now and whoever I become. But I understand if you don't want to stay here. I know that this isn't your world. It isn't your life. I would understand if you wanted to go back."

"Going back to them is the last thing that I want to do. I want to be here with you, if you'll have me. You told me that I wasn't being held captive, but I am. I'm yours, and nothing will change that. I can still see my sisters. I can still live my life. But I want to live it here with you."

Just then, Scout walked into the room and came up to me. He dropped his head onto my lap and looked up at me with his soulful eyes. I laughed, rubbing him on the head.

"And you too, of course, Scout. You saved me, too."

I looked back at Micah and found him staring at me. His eyes, those eyes that seems to have stared back at me through years, were filled with an emotion that I couldn't touch, but one that I knew I would always remember.

"From the first moment that I brought you here," he said, "I've been waiting for the moment when you would leave. I knew that I was only borrowing my time with you and I was determined to make the most of every day, every hour, every second that I had. It was like I was given another chance and even if that chance was only that I would get to talk to you and to spend time with you, I was going to be grateful for that chance and I was going to take advantage of it as much as possible. I don't want that anymore. I want to know what else this could be, because I think it could be something amazing."

"I do, too. I love you."

"I love you."

      The next day came and went. I didn't even bother to call my parents to let them know that I wasn't coming back. I was still fuming from the conversation that we had the day before and I didn't think that I had enough control over my thoughts or emotions to have a conversation with them that I wouldn't one day regret. As much as they had hurt me and as much as they continue to hurt me, they were my parents. I had to believe that somewhere, deep in their hearts, they truly did want what was best for me and thought that they we're giving that to me. Maybe someday we would talk about it again, but for now all I wanted to do was lose myself in Micah. Things had changed. Our reality was different now. We weren't together there in his lodge because we had to be. We were together because it was all that either of us wanted. I felt like I could have remained that way forever, but two days later it would all change.

      "Is he alright?" I asked into the phone.

      I was gripping it as hard as I could as if somehow that would bring me closer, make me feel less like I was helpless and out of control.

      "He's alive," my mother said. "But that's really all that we can say for now. The doctors don't know what's happening or how his body is going to react to this. You know how much trouble your father has had with his heart, Charlotte. There's no way to tell if he's going to be able to recover from this."

Tears slipped down my cheeks and I felt my hands shaking.

"What do you want me to do?" I asked.

"I think that you should come home," Violet said. "Having you gone has put a tremendous strain on him, and I know that it would do him good to have you here. If we don't know how much longer he's going to be here, then you really should be with your family."

I nodded even though I knew she couldn't see me. She was asking me to make an excruciating choice, but one that I knew I had to make.

"I'll get there as fast as I can," I said.

I was dropping the phone to the cushion beside me when Micah walked in the room.

"You'll be where as fast as you can?" he asked.

I stood up and faced him.

"My father is sick," I told him. "He's had a heart problem for a really long time and the doctors think that this last sickness weakened his heart. They don't know really how much damage has been done or if he's even going to be able to recover."

"I'm so sorry," he said.

"I need to get home," I said. "I need to get to him."

Micah nodded, though I could see the pain in his eyes.

"I know you do," he said.

"I'll only stay as long as I need to," I reassured him. "As soon as my father's better, I'll be back. I don't want to be away from you any longer than I have to."

Micah wrapped his arms around me and pulled me close. He kissed me hard as if reminding me of what was waiting for me here.

"I don't want you to be, either."

An hour later I had packed everything, said goodbye to Scout, and was on my way down the mountain with Micah. We reached the point in the access road that had been blocked by the tree and found that Madeline's car had been towed away and the tree itself had been chopped, so that the middle section was missing, creating just enough space for a truck to move through. A tree that size would take a tremendous amount of work to get out of the way and I was grateful for the effort a team had put into removing at least that section so that we could go down the road. I was nervous as we made our way down the mountain and away from the lodge. I worried that the further that we got away from the space that we had shared, the more things would change between us. I worried that the glitter would fade and by the time that we reached our hometown we would realize that things hadn't been as they had seemed.

When we got into my parents' neighborhood, however, I was still holding Micah's hand as tightly as I could and feeling him return the tightness each time I squeezed it.

"Thank you for dropping me off," I said.

"Of course," he said. "I wanted to make sure that you got here safely."

He looked up at the house as we pulled in front of it.

"This is where I lived when we were in high school," I told him.

"I wish that I had seen it then," he said.

"Me, too."

I took off my seatbelt and got out of the car, waiting as he walked around to meet me.

"Do you want me to go in with you?" he asked.

I nodded.

"I would. I know that you can't stay, but I want to have you with me as long as I can. And I want you to meet my family."

I felt my smile trembling as the thought occurred to me that this may be the only time that he was able to meet my father. All of the bitterness and anger that I had felt toward my parents sat heavily in my belly. I felt incredibly guilty for having those feelings towards them and for ever being angry or resentful toward my father. He had never been as aggressive as my mother. I couldn't imagine having him gone.

I held Micah's hand as we climbed the stairs to the front porch and I rang the doorbell. Even though this had been my home when I was younger, as soon as I moved out it started to feel distant. Every time that I came back here I felt like I was visiting and needed to announce my presence rather than just walking in. I expected one of the servants to open the door, but instead I saw my mother. The hint of a smile came to her lips for only a second and then her eyes flickered over to Micah.

"Who is this?" she asked.

"Can we come in?" I asked. "It's cold out here."

My mother seemed hesitant, but she eventually stepped aside and let us step into the house. She closed the door and turned another suspicious glare toward Micah.

"Who is this?" she asked again.

"This is the man I was telling you about," I said. "This is Micah Davis."

I didn't expect that she would recognize the name, but the darkness that rolled over her face as soon as I said it told me that she did. Her eyes narrowed and her back straightened.

"Micah Davis?" she growled. "What are you doing bringing a person like this into my home?"

My face fell, and I felt my heart start to pound in my chest.

"What do you mean a person like this?" I asked.

"Don't think I don't remember who he is," my mother snapped. "He's that boy who never learned his place in high school.

He came from a disreputable family and had the nerve to walk into your school and steal the popularity and respect from boys who really deserved it. They never should have let someone like him on the football team or allowed him to take advantage of the same opportunities as the boys from the good families."

I couldn't believe what my mother was saying. I couldn't believe that she would stand there and look Micah directly in the eye as she said such horrible things about him.

"Stop it, Mother."

"Why should I?" she asked. "It's not like he doesn't know. He knows exactly who he is and what he did. It serves him right what he went through in college. He never belonged in the world of society anyway."

"You're right," Micah said. "I never belonged around people like you."

He turned toward me and ducked his head to kiss me goodbye. I wanted to ask him to stay, but I also didn't want to subject him to another minute in that house. He walked out, his shoulders square and his fists clenched by his side but in complete control of himself. I whipped around to face my mother.

"What's wrong with you?" I asked. "How dare you say things like that to him? Do you have any idea what he went through or what he's accomplished?"

"None of that matters," my mother said. "All that matters is the family that he was born into and the type of person his father was."

I wanted to point out just how hypocritical she was and how ridiculous she sounded, but I didn't have it in me. The anger and frustration that I was feeling move becoming like a dagger through my heart and I knew if I stood there with her for any longer I would never get to my father. I glared at her a final time and then started up the stairs towards my parents' bedroom. I walked in the room to see my father lying in bed, blanket pulled up nearly to his chest.

"Daddy," I said.

It had been so long since I had called him that, but in that moment, it was the only thing that sounded appropriate.

"Charlotte," he said. "It's good to see you home. Your mother tells me that you were in some house on the mountain with a man. Are you alright? Did he do anything to you?"

"No," I said shaking my head. "He didn't do anything to me. He didn't kidnap me. I was there because I wanted to be. But now I'm here and I'll be here as long as you need me."

They were some of the most painful words that I had ever said.

Chapter Fifteen

Micah

I wanted to destroy things. I craved violence and vengeance like I never had in my life, and the feeling was unsettling. It was a part of me that I had kept buried deep within me my entire life, a part of me that I felt as though I had been born with and couldn't avoid, that I could control. There have been so few times in my entire life when I had felt that level of rage come forward toward another person. It had been there when I had seen my father attack my mother. It had been there when I had seen Daniel hurt Charlotte in the hall of the high school. It had been there to a lesser degree when I found out that Helen was sleeping with my best friend. Now it felt as though it were threatening to consume me and all I could do is struggle to keep it down.

I couldn't believe what Charlotte's mother had said about me. As soon as that thought came to my mind though, I knew that it was wrong. I could absolutely believe what she had said to me. It was exactly what all of the other guys had said that she felt and believed. It was exactly what would have happened in high school had I ever shown Charlotte even for a second that I was interested in her. It didn't matter to her that I was now a successful adult with wealth that far eclipsed hers many times over. All she saw when she looked at me was that same boy for whom she had so much disdain. Now I didn't even have Charlotte in my arms and I had to deal with the fact that she was there in that house with them. Her love for her father and her worry about him had convinced her to sacrifice her own comfort and happiness to make sure that she could be there for him. It was part of what I loved about her. But it was also what I hated about them.

The lodge felt desolate without her. It had always been empty. I had known from the moment that I started designing it that it would be home to me and to Scout, but to no one else. It was intended to be empty, but it never felt that way until Charlotte walked out of it. Now it seemed as though every inch of it was pressing down around me, making it harder to breathe. I wanted to hear her voice again. I wanted to see her sitting by the fire consuming the books as fast as she could or at the kitchen table nibbling her way through whatever she had prepared for the day. I wanted to see her sleep, peaceful and indescribably beautiful. I wanted to feel her skin and her breath on me. I needed her back here with me.

****

Charlotte

"I can't believe you would say something like that. "

"You have to admit it's a strange story," Miranda said.

"I don't care what you think," I said. "You have no right to say that he did something wrong."

"He had you up in his house for two weeks," my sister said. "You didn't even call us to let us know that you were alright."

"And none of you even called to report me missing. None of you thought for a second that I could be in any type of danger, and now all of a sudden you are so worried about me?"

"You've done this before," she said.

"Mom said the same thing," I said. "What are you talking about?"

"Are you seriously going to pretend that you don't know?"

"I don't know."

"Daniel told us about how you and he got into an argument and you stormed out of his apartment and disappeared for a week while you were in college. He said that was why we didn't hear from you and that he spent the whole week desperately looking for you because he was so worried. He said that when he found you, you are in some strange man's apartment and had obviously been drinking and probably more."

Spots danced in front of my eyes and I felt my fists clenched.

"You actually believe that? You actually believe that that happened? You think that if I was missing no one else would notice? He's supposedly so worried about me, but he doesn't even call my parents to let them know that I've just wandered off? Do you realize how asinine that sounds?"

"It's normal to protect yourself when you are in a dangerous situation by pretending that you're happy and that you're having a good time. It happens to a lot of kidnapping victims."

"I am not a kidnapping victim," I said, enunciating the words as carefully as I could to make sure that she heard each of them. "Micah rescued me. He is the only one who cared what happened to me during that storm and he's the one who kept me safe. If he had kidnapped me, do you really think that he would have brought me back here so easily?"

"You got the phone and you called Mom," she said. "He knew that there were now people who knew what had happened and where you were. It's not like he could just keep you and think that no one was going to notice that."

I shook my head.

"You're unbelievable," I said. "All of you are unbelievable. You don't understand and don't listen to me when I'm trying to tell you that I'm in a miserable and abusive relationship, but then when I find someone who actually loves me and who is wonderful to me, you're suddenly up in arms and think that I'm in some sort of danger. You're all being ridiculous. I wish that I had never come back."

I ran up the stairs toward the bedroom that I had slept in my entire life. It was one thing that I had to give my mother credit for. She had never changed it. Not even after I left home. Not even after I went to college and told her that I was starting my own life. Not even over the years that I had lived in my own apartment. This room it always remained exactly as it has been. It was my room and it always would be. I was nearly to it when I heard my father calling me. I walked into the study and found him sitting in one of the large leather chairs next to the window. The room reminded me of the library and Micah's lodge and my heart squeezed.

"Daddy," I said, "you shouldn't be out of bed."

I hoped that if I focused again on my father it would help to ease the pain that I was feeling. If I reminded myself of why I had walked away from Micah and justify every moment until I was able to be with him again.

"I'm all right," my father said. "All I'm doing is sitting here. What was all that yelling I heard?"

"It was nothing," I said.

"Don't lie to me, little girl. What's going on down there?"

"I was just having an argument with Miranda."

"About what?"

"I don't really want to talk about it, Daddy."

"Tell me," he said.

"She thinks that the man who saved me from the storm kidnapped me and mistreated me."

"Did he?"

"No. no, Daddy. Micah would never do anything like that. He's an incredible man and I love him."

"What about Daniel?"

I let out a long sigh and squeezed my eyes closed.

"I don't want to hear about Daniel anymore," I said. "That's over. It's been over. It will always be over. I don't love him. I don't want to be with him."

I started toward the door, but turned around just before walking out of it.

"Is there anything that I can get for you, Daddy?"

He shook his head.

"No."

****

Micah

"Come back," I said. "I'll come get you now. Just come home."

"I wish I could," Charlotte said.

Her voice sounded different over the phone. It was thinner, losing some of the depth and sweetness that I loved to hear so much.

"What's stopping you?" I asked.

"My father is still sick," she said. "The doctors don't know what's wrong, I'm worried about leaving him."

"I understand. I know that you're worried about him and you don't want to leave him. But you sound miserable."

"I am miserable," she told me. "I miss you so much. I hate being here and being away from you everyday. I hate trying so hard to get along with my mother and my sisters and hearing the things that they say. I wish that they knew you."

"They don't need to know me," I said. "All that matters is that you know me."

"That's not all that matters," she said. "You don't deserve to have them talk about you the way that they do. They have no idea who you are. They've never known who you are. The worst part about it is that I expect this from my mother. I love her and there are times when she is really a good person, but one of her greatest flaws is the way that she looks at other people. It's a way for her to feel better about herself and to deflect the way people look at her. I've always known that about her. But I didn't expect it from Miranda."

"They just want to protect you" I said.

"You're the only one who has ever really protected me."

"When are you coming home?"

"As soon as I can."

I let the phone drop from my fingers onto the table in front of me and stared at it as it spun around lazily. Before that phone call it had been 3 days since I had spoken to Charlotte and it felt like far too much. I couldn't just sit around and wait for her any longer. I had walked away from her because of the way that her mother had talked about me, but I wasn't going to do it again. I wasn't going to let her have that control over me or over Charlotte. I was going to take matters into my own hands and make sure that the woman I loved knew where she belonged. I needed to make sure that she knew how much I truly cared about her and that I was willing to do whatever it took to make sure that we could have the future together that we both wanted. Even if that meant putting aside my anger and sitting down with her parents to tell them how much I love Charlotte, that I could take care of her, and that I wanted to spend my life doing anything that I needed to, to make their daughter happy.

I headed out of the house and toward town. Toward Charlotte.

I was nearly to Charlotte's parents' house when I turned into the small parking lot in front of the florist. I realized that I had never brought Charlotte flowers and somehow that simple gesture seemed incredibly important, like it was something that I needed to do. I walked into the shop and began to explore the refrigerators full of blooms that lined the walls. There was something so incredibly strange and unnatural about seeing these flowers in their full, pristine condition just a matter of days before Christmas. I didn't see anything that seemed to fit Charlotte and decided that I should speak to the florist. I was heading toward the front counter when I heard a familiar voice. I paused, glancing around the edge of a display to see Charlotte's mother and a man walk-in. He was a taller, older version of the boy I had seen in the hallway with her so many years before and I knew instantly that it was Daniel.

"I can't tell you how happy this is making me," Charlotte's mother said.

"And you're sure you don't mind that it will be at your Christmas party?" Daniel asked.

"Of course not! What could be more perfect than a surprise proposal at Christmas? Everyone that Charlotte knows, and loves will be there, and she'll get to share this joyous moment with them."

I felt my stomach drop. He was going to propose to her.

"I've been looking forward to this for so long," Daniel said. "I can't wait to finally make her my wife."

"I'm just so glad that she finally saw the light and has forgiven you. I know this is been so hard for you, but she, I'm sure, is going to make it up to you. I'm just so thrilled. I know that this is all going to work out so perfectly."

The world around me seem to go red for an instant and my fingers tightened around the display in front of me until I could feel the metal cutting into my skin. Fury burned in my belly and I could taste bile rising up my throat and into my mouth. Charlotte had forgiven him. She had gone back to him and now she was going to marry him. She was no better than Helen. I had opened myself up to her. I had allowed myself to be vulnerable again and to feel things that I had pushed away for so long, and she betrayed me. I stalked down the aisle and out of the shop, not caring if either saw me. I just wanted to get back home to the lodge and pretend that the last few weeks hadn't even happened. I wanted to push through Christmas and let the new year ahead of me blur the memories that I had of Charlotte and of ever thinking that things could be different.

Chapter Sixteen

Charlotte

I tried to put down the phone before Miranda saw me holding it, but I knew by the look on her face that she had seen me. She had also seen me brush away the tear that sat on my cheek from yet again having the phone ring incessantly before going to voicemail.

"Did you call him again?" she asked, doing nothing to conceal the judgment in her voice.

There's no point in trying to deny it. She knew that I had called Micah more than a dozen times every day for the last two days. He hasn't answered any of them.

"I just don't understand," I said.

"We tried to explain it to you," she said. "We told you that everything was going to be different after you had been home for a while."

"But he said..."

"And I'm sure he said that to plenty of people before."

I shook my head. I didn't want to believe it. I didn't want to let myself even think for a second that everything that he had said to me had been a lie, no matter what my mother or my older sister was trying to tell me.

"It doesn't make any sense," I said.

"Of course, it does. He had fun with you while he could and now it's over. The romance and drama of it was fun while it lasted, but after a few days it passed, and you don't amuse him anymore. You just have to face it, Charlotte. He doesn't want anything to do with you anymore. You need to stop trying. Stop throwing yourself at him. It's not going to change anything and it's just going to make you look more pathetic."

I looked up at my sister.

"Thank you so much for that," I said. "I really appreciate all the love and support that you're showing me."

Miranda sighed and sat down beside me, wrapping an arm around me.

"Sarcasm has never really been a good color on you, Charlotte. But I'm sorry anyway. I really don't mean to be hurting your feelings. I care so much about you and I just want to see you be happy. I want you to know what it's like to have what I have. A husband. A home. Children. A real life. That man isn't going to give it to you, so you need to just put him behind you and move on."

"I'll try," I said.

Miranda hopped up and offered me her hand.

"Come on," she said. "There's no time like the present. We have a Christmas party to get ready for and nothing helps to soothe a broken heart like getting festive."

I tried to laugh. She looked as excited as a small child that it was Christmas season and I knew that she was looking forward to my parents' party. The party was always a time for her to show off a new outfit, or how perfectly her children were dressed, or the new piece of jewelry that her husband had gotten for her. This year, it was an opportunity for her to talk about being pregnant and to rub the very tiny burgeoning belly that still was at the phase where it looked like she had just eaten a little bit too much. I wasn't looking forward to the party as much. I wanted to be excited for Christmas. I wanted to be happy that my father seemed to be recovering. But my heart was aching for Micah and I couldn't make it stop. My mother and my sisters had told me that I was being ridiculous thinking that I ever could have had anything with him. They said that it was crazy for me to even think that things could have worked out between us. We were from two different worlds and no matter how much I didn't want it to, that mattered.

I struggled to believe that. I thought about the days that had passed when I lost my memory. I didn't know who I was then or anything that had happened to me in the past. I didn't know who my family was or who Micah was. And yet I had felt such a strong connection to him. I felt such a powerful pull to him, as if something inside of me was reaching out to him for recognition and for safety. Again, I thought about how my life seemed to have orbited his. I had been so attracted to him even before I started dating Daniel, and then while we were together I still couldn't stop myself from thinking about him or wanting to find ways to be close to him. I wish that there was something that could have been different. Just a single moment. Maybe if he had turned around one day and said something to me when he saw me rather than just walking away. Maybe if I'd have been brave enough to actually try to be a part of the popular crowd rather than just staying on the outer edge all the time. Maybe if I had taken one of the opportunities to say something to him. Maybe if I hadn't let my shyness and insecurity shape everything about myself and how I saw the world around me. Maybe even if I had just chased after Micah that afternoon, followed him just long enough to say thank you for protecting me from Daniel. Maybe then life would have been different.

Miranda walked out of the room and I followed her, knowing in the back of my mind that nothing she had said had changed my thoughts or my heart. I was going to push my way through the Christmas party. I was going to smile like they expected me to. I was going to greet our guests and try to be as festive and happy as I possibly could be. But as soon as it was over I was going back to the mountain. I was going home to Micah.

I could hear the party in full swing below me as I put the finishing touch on my hair and gave my lips a final swipe of red lipstick. I wanted to look perfect. Not for the party, but so that when I left I could go straight to Micah. I heard my mother call up to me and I told her that I was on my way. I slipped into my high heels as I walked out of the room, feeling happier and more excited than I had in days. As soon as I got to the middle of the staircase, however, all of that disappeared. Daniel was standing at the bottom of the steps looking up at me. My mother was standing to one side of him, a smile on her face. I knew that this has been planned. I knew that this was not a surprise to her. She knew that he was coming, and she didn't tell me. The guests had started to trickle toward the entryway, but I didn't care. I took another few steps toward him, glaring directly into Daniels eyes.

"What are you doing here?" I asked.

"I was invited."

I felt like I was right back in the cabin. I felt like this was the conversation that we had already had, and it is all starting over again. My mind was swimming. I was furious, but I was also afraid. I didn't understand how this could be happening again.

"I didn't invite you. I don't want you here."

"Charlotte, don't act this way," my mother said. "There are guests here."

She was still grinning, almost maniacally, as if somehow, she can make it so the people around her didn't hear her scolding me as long as she was smiling.

"I don't care that they're our guests here, mother. I do care that he's here. I made it very clear that I didn't want to see him again. How dare you invite him here and not tell me?"

"I don't need to get permission from you to invite anyone to my own house," she said.

"Fine," I said. "But you could at least show me the respect of not having him here when I have told you that I don't want to see him. I have told you again and again that our relationship is over."

"Charlotte, please," Daniel said. "Don't be mad at your mother. I asked her if I could come here. I needed to see you again. And I thought that this party would be the perfect opportunity because I have come here for a very special reason. I've come here to bare my soul to you, to look you in the eye and tell you but there is nothing in this world that is as precious to me as you, and that I can't imagine another day of my life without you."

"Daniel, stop."

Daniel reached into his pocket and pulled out a black velvet box. I couldn't believe that this was happening. I gripped the banister beside me, trying to keep myself calm, trying to keep myself under control.

"Charlotte Dabney, I have loved you for so long and I want to keep loving you. Will you marry me?"

Gasps rose up through the crowd as if the guests had the same bizarre filter as my mother and hadn't heard the confrontation between Daniel and me. Instead, they had only heard the proposal and were somehow wrapped up in what they saw as the romance of it all.

"Daniel, I didn't come back here for you. I came back here to take care of my father."

"To take care of me?" my father asked.

"She doesn't really mean that," my mother said hastily, patting my father on the back, trying to guide him back into the living room with the rest of the guests. "She just means that she's happy that she's home so that you can spend more time with you."

I narrowed my eyes at my mother.

"That's not what I mean. I mean that my mother called me and told me that my father was extremely ill, and the doctors didn't know if he was going to survive because of his weakened heart. She told me that I needed to come home so that I could help take care of him and be here with him because it might be his last few weeks."

"Violet, is this true?" my father asked.

In that moment I realized that I had never once mentioned this to my father. I had tried to keep it from him because I thought that talking about his illness would only be more difficult for him.

"You have been sick," my mother said.

"I had the flu," my father said. "That's all. I was already nearly recovered by the time that she got here. The doctors didn't say anything to me about my heart or about this weakening me in any way."

"What's going on?" I asked.

I saw my mother and Daniel exchange glances and realization settled over me. They had done this on purpose. She had lured me back to her so that she could offer me up to Daniel.

"I don't know how to make this any more clear for either one of you," I said, no longer afraid. "I want nothing to do with Daniel. I want nothing to do with a man who is cruel and abusive and manipulative and neglectful. What I do want is the man who I love with everything in me. And who loves me in return."

"Who is she talking about?" Daniel demanded.

"You didn't tell him?" I asked, then turned to look at Daniel. "When I left you in the cabin the week of Thanksgiving I was rescued from the storm by the most amazing man I have ever met. And it turns out I met him before I thought I did. His name is Micah Davis and we've known him since high school. He rescued me and took care of me."

"He kidnapped her," my mother insisted. "He took her and kept her in his lodge and didn't let her call home and didn't let her try to get help."

"That's not true," I said. "None of you looked for me. None of you cared that I was missing."

"We didn't think it was possible that you could be in the hands of such a dangerous man."

"There's nothing dangerous about Micah. He is more successful and powerful than any of you. And he did that for himself. He didn't just grab onto the coattails of his father and ride them to a life of complacency. He created himself into the man he is today and there is no other man in this world who I could ever imagine spending a single day with."

I started back up the stairs to my room, wanting to change my clothes and pack my bags. I didn't care anymore what anyone thought. I was nearly to the top of the stairs when I heard Daniel's voice calling up to me.

"You're throwing your life away if you walk away from me and go back to him."

I paused and turned around slowly to look at him.

"No, Daniel. That's what I would be doing if I stayed with you. If I survived at all."

There was a car following me as I got onto the access road that led up a mountain to Micah's House.

It was too close.

It wasn't just on the same road as me, it was following me.

I tried to go a little faster. I tried to ignore it. But it was still there.

I looked in my rearview mirror as the car behind me crept even closer and realized that it was Daniel behind the wheel. He was glaring at me and even at that distance, I could see that his eyes were dark and emotionless, as if there was nothing behind them but hatred. He pulled up closer behind until I couldn't even see the front of his car. I worried that he was going to ram me, and I pressed down on the gas a little more. I didn't want to go too fast. I knew from personal experience just how treacherous this road could be, and I knew that it got more dangerous, narrower and curvier, the higher it went on the mountain.

Going faster could just put me in more danger. Going faster would mean that I wouldn't be able to control the car if he did get close enough to hit me. But going faster could also mean that I could get away from him. It could also mean that I might have the opportunity to find my way to Micah's house and into the safety of the lodge and his arms before Daniel could get to me.

All of the fear that I had pushed away since I had been standing on the steps in my parents' house, looking down at him, suddenly surged back. He knew now that he was never going to get his way. He knew now that I had moved on with my life that he wasn't going to be able to manipulate his way back. For all of those years he had been the center of my life, whether I wanted him to be or not. He knew that he had strategically and carefully manipulated me until I had nothing else, until I was fully isolated from everything and everyone so there was nothing else to keep me distracted from him. He knew that, in all that time that we were apart, I had almost nothing and that made it easier for him to convince me to take him back. That wasn't the way that it was anymore. I had Micah now. I had a life. And I wasn't going to give it up for him.

Though as I glanced back through the rearview mirror at him again, the fear coursed through me and I realized that he didn't want me to give up my life for him. He wanted to take it from me.

The closer that we got to Micah's House, the more I thought about Daniel and his motivations. I didn't understand why he would be following me, but then it occurred to me that it wasn't just me he wanted to get to. He would probably be satisfied with destroying me, but if he could also take down the man who had led to his humiliation, he would gladly do that as well. I couldn't let him do that. I couldn't lead him directly to Micah, knowing how much danger I would be putting the man I loved in.

I watch the road in front of me carefully, looking out for the specific milestones that I wanted to find. Finally, I saw them, and I knew that just up ahead would be the tree. I didn't know if the team had been working on it and had cleared more of it away. I hoped that they hadn't. I needed there to still be part of the tree there. I came around the bend and my heart lifted slightly when I saw that the majority of the mass of tree was still laying across the road. The section that had been removed to allow clear passage didn't seem any bigger, which was perfect. I pressed on the gas so that I shot ahead and into the passage. As soon as I did, I took my foot off the gas and turned the wheel so that my car slid around to come across the road. It was an incredibly risky move. If I had done it wrong I would have gone tumbling down the mountain. When the car finally settled, and I realized that it had worked out exactly as I had intended it to, I let out a breath and quickly fought my way out of my seat belt. I scrambled out of the car and started up the ridge.

The way that my car was positioned now meant that Daniel wouldn't be able to get through and up the access road. If he wanted to chase me, he was going to have to do it on foot. I could hear the explosive sound of Daniel slamming his car door, but I was already most of the way up the ridge. There was another incredibly loud sound and then a sharper sound beside me. I screamed as I realized that he had just shot at me. I forced myself up the rocks faster, trying to remember the way that Micah had led me. I wasn't wearing the right clothes. I hadn't taken the time to put on all of the layers that I should have. But I was wearing boots and they gripped just enough to get me up and over and soon I was running through the trees. I looked down as I ran, trying to find footsteps that would guide me up to the lodge. The cold temperatures had ensured that the snow hasn't melted, and I was able to find a track that it only been partially obliterated by animals. I followed it, pushing myself through the snow drift as fast as I possibly could. I could hear Daniel chasing behind me, he occasionally screamed my name and there was a tone in it, something new and terrifying, that shot through my heart and made it difficult to breathe.

I followed the footsteps for several hundred yards, and then I veered off. If I had continued to follow those footsteps it would have led directly to the lodge, and directly to Micah. I didn't know where I was going as I continued to run through the trees, but I knew that I was putting distance between myself and the house. That was putting distance between Daniel and the house. I would figure something out, but all I cared about was that I could keep that gun away from Micah.

"You're never going to get away from me, Charlotte" Daniel shouted from behind me. "You've tried your whole life to get away from me and you never have. You never will."

I heard another shot and I clamped my hand over my mouth to keep from screaming. I glanced over my shoulder and couldn't see him, and realized that meant that he couldn't see me. He was taunting me, trying to get me to say something so that he would be able to find my location. If I could stay quiet and continue to the trees there was a possibility that I could lose him and then backtrack and find my way to the lodge again. I knew that the air up here was frigidly cold, but I didn't feel it. There was too much adrenaline and fire in my blood, pumping through my body, for me to feel anything but the urge to run.

I took a sharp turn and quickly realized that it was the wrong move. Daniel was yards ahead of me and he turned just in time to see me before I ducked behind a tree. Another bullet whizzed past me and I shot out from behind the tree, continuing to run.

A sudden thought occurred to me and I took a moment to try to orient myself. I remembered the day that I had spent out on the property with Micah and the emergency shelter that he had shown me. This is one of the most important features of the house that he had designed, he told me. He had made sure that that shelter was designed to withstand virtually anything. It would keep him safe from any type of severe weather, earthquakes, even a wildfire. It had enough supplies in it to support him and Scout for over a month. The most important thing about it, however, was that it had a thick heat and pressure resistant door on the outside and a tunnel that led to the lodge on the inside. If I could get to that emergency shelter and get inside, I would be able to lock the door and prevent Daniel from getting to me. Then I could go through the tunnel to the lodge. Even if the door to the tunnel was locked, I knew that there was an emergency phone down there and I would be able to call Micah.

I felt confident that I had figured out the way to get to the shelter and I ran as hard as I could. My legs had begun to burn, and I felt that my muscles were beginning to give out on me. I was having trouble drawing enough air into my lungs and my head was starting to swim. It felt like I was crying, but my tears were freezing on my cheeks. Suddenly I felt something hard hit me in the back of the head and I cried out as I fell forward onto my hands and knees. I looked to the side and saw a small rock sitting in the snow. I turned over and looked up just in time to see Daniel appear over me. He had been holding the gun to his side but now he lifted it up and pointed it directly at me. There was a maniacal smile on his face and I barely even recognized him. I wondered how many times I had fed into this. How many times had I contributed to the monster that was growing inside him. The sound of Micah's voice reverberated through my mind.

You didn't deserve this. You didn't do anything wrong. There was nothing that you did that made him that way.

"Why are you doing this, Daniel?" I asked, feeling stronger now.

"Don't be stupid," he said. "I've always hated when you acted like you were stupid."

"I want you to tell me," I said.

"You should have just said yes. You have no idea how lucky you are. You have no idea how many women would do anything to be in your place."

I was getting incredibly tired of being told how lucky I was to be tormented.

"Then why didn't you just choose one of them?" I asked. "If there are so many others who want you, why didn't you just choose another one? Why me?"

"Because I don't want any of them. I want you. You are the one that I picked out in high school and that means that you are the one that I want. That means you are who I am going to have. And if I can't have you, then no one else is going to."

I saw his finger move on the gun, but before he could pull the trigger, I heard him cry out. I didn't know what had happened, but when I scrambled to my feet I saw that Daniel was on the snow, his hand gripping his leg. He was glaring ahead of him and I looked to see Scout standing there, baring his teeth in a way that I had never seen him before.

"Scout" I cried out.

Daniel was getting to his feet and I saw that Scout had bitten his leg, tearing through his pants and scraping his skin. He took a lunging step toward the dog, before he could get to him a massive figure came out of the trees and landed on him. It was Micah, who pushed up from Daniel and punched him in the face. Daniel tried to fight back, but Micah grabbed the fist that came toward him and punched him again. Daniel was lying still now, and Micah got off of him, turning around to look at me.

"Are you alright?" he asked.

"He had a gun," I told him. "Where is it?"

Micah and I looked around and I saw the gun a few feet away. He reached to get it and out of the corner of my eye I saw Daniel standing up. His hand was lifted nearly over his head and I saw that he was gripping a knife. It glinted in the moonlight and I screamed just before he brought it down, plunging it deep into Micah's back. Micah reared back and roared with the pain, but then whirled around and knocked the knife out of Daniel's hand. It skittered across the frozen surface of the snow and landed just a few feet from me. I snatched it up and brought it close to me so that Daniel couldn't get it again. The two men were grappling now, fighting fiercely as both struggled for dominance over the other. Scout lunged in and bit Daniel again, tearing away a chunk of his skin.

Micah managed to get Daniel on his back and was holding him down when he turned to look at me over his shoulder.

"Charlotte, go to the lodge. Call the police. Scout show her the way."

I didn't want to go. I didn't want to leave Micah, but I knew that we needed help. I reached for my cell phone, thinking that I could call and still stay with him, but then I realized that I had left my phone in the car. Scout was next to me now as I stood. As soon as I was on my feet he took off, nearly disappearing into the darkness. I chased him, relying on the light from the moon and the stars to bounce off of the white patches on him so that I could keep him in sight, as he led me to the lodge. I had only been running for a few seconds when I heard a gunshot split the night air around me.

Chapter Seventeen

Charlotte

I sat beside a hospital bed the next afternoon, holding Micah's hand and staring into his face. There was still blood splattered on my clothes from where I tried to hold him when we are riding in the ambulance on the way to the hospital. I didn't care. I wasn't going to leave until he was awake. The doctors had spent hours working on him, but he had gotten through the surgery and they said that he was doing well. I had never felt such incredible gratitude as I had in that moment. I was grateful to the team of doctors who had worked so hard to save him, and I was grateful to Micah for literally putting his life on the line for me.

I felt in that moment, more than any other moment in my life, more than when I was going through anything else that I had ever faced, that the true horror of Daniel was really illuminated. In that moment I saw more than I ever had before, the impact of what I had suffered at his hands, and how far-reaching that impact could really be. It wasn't just the way that he had treated me. It was that I had made the decision, over and over again, to continue putting myself in that place and allowing that treatment to continue, and to worsen. I made the decision over and over again to stay with him. I knew now that there was nothing that I did that made me deserve the way that he treated me, and it was in no way my fault, but he had always managed to make me feel as though it were. He made me feel as though I deserved the way that he was treating me and like I would never be able to find someone who wouldn't treat me that way. It had gotten to the point where I felt like maybe he was right. Like maybe this was inevitable, it was just something that I was going to have to deal with. There was a small part of me that believed that maybe, in some way, everyone dealt with this.

But I knew that that wasn't the case. I knew that my mother never had to deal with treatment like this from my father. I knew that neither of my sisters ever had to deal with anything like this from their husbands. None of them had ever experienced what I had, and that it was part of what had made them unable to see what I was going through and how serious it really was. There was a part of me though that believed that it was me. There's something about me that attracted the type of man who would treat a woman that way. If that were the case, if it was something about me, then there was no point in trying to escape Daniel because I would only find myself in the same position again and again. At least with Daniel, I knew him. I knew the look in his eye and how to gauge his emotions and his moods. I knew what he looked like when he was angry. I knew what it looked like when he was tired. I knew what he looked like when someone had said something to piss him off or when he had been disappointed or overlooked. I knew those sides of him and what to expect when I saw those looks. Though it didn't protect me, it prepared me, in a way that was far preferable to what could be waiting for me with another man.

But now I knew what was waiting for me with another man. It was sheer happiness and contentment. It was the feeling of being safe, adored, and loved. It was the knowledge that he would keep me safe and would never hurt me. That was what made this moment, as I sat by the bed and held his hand, waiting for when his eyes would open again, so painful and difficult. This was the moment that illuminated how bad that relationship really was and the fact that it wasn't just me that it affected. Up until now I believed that I was the only one who Daniel would hurt. I was the only one he had ever done anything to. He was arrogant, conceited, snobby, and elitist. He thought that he was better than virtually everyone around him and was known to be dismissive and even mean to those who he saw as beneath him. But he was in good company in that behavior. Unfortunately, that was not unusual in our world. I hated it, but it wasn't violent. It wasn't cruel. It wasn't dangerous. Now, though, that had completely changed. Daniel had now brutally injured someone else. The man I loved. I was overcome with guilt, but there was another feeling deep inside me, a feeling that I welcomed, and that I knew was never going to change. I was utterly, passionately devoted to Micah.

****

Micah

Charlotte was sitting beside my hospital bed when I opened my eyes. Feeling her hand wrapped around mine and having her face be the first thing I saw was the most wonderful moment that I could have imagined. I wasn't entirely sure what had happened as I looked around.

"Where am I?" I asked.

She laughed.

"Do you know who you are?" she asked.

I nodded.

"Yes," I said.

"Then I still have you beat," she said.

Though she was doing her best to smile and laugh, I could see the tears in her eyes and the streaks down her cheeks created by hours of crying. She was now gripping my hand with both of hers and leaning forward onto the bed. It was as if she was trying to get as close to me as she possibly could.

"What happened? I don't really remember much after Scout brought me outside and I heard you screaming."

"Scout was amazing," I told him. "He saved me. You could probably go ahead and start calling him Lassie now."

I laughed and felt a sharp pain go through my back and my stomach. I groaned loudly.

"I don't think that he would like that very much," I said.

"He probably would," she said. "But he did. He saved me. Daniel had come after me with a gun. He was trying to kill me, but Scout bit him and he dropped the gun. The two of you fought and he stabbed you in the back. I was heading for the lodge to call for help when I heard a gunshot. I found out that he shot you in the stomach while you were fighting."

I drew in a breath as I tried to process it

"Did they find him?" I asked.

Charlotte nodded.

"Before you passed out you managed to hit him one more time and it knocked him unconscious. You were both lying there in the snow when the police came. They brought him here and fixed him up a little, but now he's at the jail. He'll be away for a long time."

"Good," I said. That's when I noticed the blood on her clothes.

"Did he hurt you?" I asked.

I didn't care about what I had gone through. All that mattered to me was whether she had been hurt.

"No," she said. "This is your blood. I brought the police to you and when I saw you all I wanted to do was hold you. Your eyes were closed, and you were just laying there. There was blood in the snow. I thought..."

Her breath caught, and she looked down. I felt a tear hit my hand and saw her shoulders shaking.

"Shh," I said, trying to soothe her. "I'm here. I'm right here. I'm going to be fine."

"You rescued me again," she said. "One of these days you are going to get tired of having to come to my rescue."

"Never," I said. "I will never stop wanting to rescue you. I just hope that you won't have many more things that you need to be rescued from."

"I'm so sorry that you had to go through this," she said.

I shook my head again.

"I would do it again. I would do all of it again. I feel like this is the culmination of everything that I have gone through. Everything that I have suffered in my life has been worth it, because it culminated in me being there in those moments to save you. I only wish that we hadn't waited so long. I wish that I had known you more and that we could have spent more of our lives together."

"Maybe we would have been able to protect each other."

I reached up and cupped her cheek with my hand, stroking across her cheek bone with my thumb.

"What has happened has happened," I told her. "There's nothing that we can do to change it. All that we can do is change every moment going forward. We will never be able to go back and make those things go away, but we can make sure that nothing like that ever happens again. We can make every moment of the rest of our lives so incredible that they drown out every one from the past. I don't regret any of it. I will never regret any of it."

"You sound like you think I'm going away," she said.

"I didn't know how you were feeling anymore, I don't want you to feel like you are being forced to do anything ever again."

Charlotte smiled and brought my hand forward to press against her heart.

"I'm not being forced to do anything. I never want to be away from you again. You're never getting rid of me."

"Even if you forget who you are again?" I asked, a slight laugh in my voice.

"Even if I forget who I am again," she said. "My heart didn't forget you this time and it won't ever again."

Epilogue

Charlotte

"You really should have stayed in the hospital for a little bit longer," I said.

I had my arm wrapped around Micah's waist and was carefully helping him over to the sofa in the great room. He dropped down onto the cushions and let out a sigh. I wasn't sure if it was a sigh of relief or in response to pain in his still healing wounds.

"Absolutely not," he said. "A measly little gunshot and stab wound aren't going to keep me from celebrating our first Christmas together."

"I didn't know that you liked Christmas so much" I said.

"Well, I didn't really until you came along."

"Why is that?" I asked mischievously.

"Maybe because you are the best thing that Santa has ever brought me."

I looked over at the incredible tree that filled one side of the room. I had never seen a Christmas tree that big and it was truly breathtaking.

"How did you manage to get a tree like that in here? You've only been home from the hospital for six hours and I was only getting two of your prescriptions filled.

"Scout helped me," Micah said.

I laughed.

"Scout helped you go out into the woods, pick a tree, chop it down, and set it up in the lodge?"

"All of this rescue stuff has given him a new sense of confidence," he said. "He believes he can do anything now."

I looked over at the dog who was sprawled in front of the fire, shamelessly turning his belly toward the warmth of the flames.

"Somehow, I just don't believe that that's true," I said.

"Alright," Micah said. "I might have had a little bit of help."

"A couple of little Santa's helpers all your own?"

"Something like that. Come on out the jig is up."

I looked in the direction that he was calling and saw Madeline, Miranda, William, and Seth come into the room. My sisters were carrying boxes of decorations and all were smiling happily.

"Direct from the North Pole," Miranda said.

I grinned, crossing the room to my sisters and gathering both of them in hugs.

"What are you doing here?" I asked.

"Micah told us that he wanted a little bit of Christmas magic in the lodge," Madeline said.

"But since he is just a touch incapacitated at the moment, we offered to give him a hand," William said.

I was nearly overwhelmed by the happiness that filled me. In the days following Daniel's attack, each of my sisters had come to me and apologized. They told me exactly what I had suspected, that they didn't even know what I had been going through. They had heard a few rumors and thought that they had overheard me when I tried to tell Mom what I'd been experiencing with Daniel, but they didn't believe it. They never knew the full extent. They felt horrible about it, but I couldn't blame them. How could I possibly hold them accountable for not understanding what I was going through and for doing nothing to stand up for me, when for so long I didn't understand what I was doing to myself? I was just so happy to have my sisters back and to know that they accepted Micah and my desire for a future with him.

"Thanks for your help," Micah said. "So, what do you think? Should we start decorating?"

"Absolutely," I said.

"If a couple of my little helpers don't mind, there's some eggnog and cookies in the kitchen."

"OK," Madeline said as she walked to the great room and into the kitchen, "I think we got a little bit too far with Santa's Little Helpers thing."

"Never," Micah said.

He pulled himself slowly off of the couch and started toward the boxes of decorations that my sisters had put down. He started pulling out containers of glass balls and tinsel in shades of burgundy and gold. Seth and William had already gone to work trying to wind strands of lights around the enormous tree and for a moment it looked as though I might lose one of my brothers-in-law to the branches. Madeline and Miranda came back into the room carrying the eggnog and cookies. Micah gestured at them.

"See? Regular elves."

Both sisters laughed and set the treats on a table up against one wall. We started hanging the decorations and after a few minutes Micah offered me one that looked slightly different from the others. It was a round burgundy ball with gold accents, but a band around the middle made it look as though it could open. I took the ball in both hands and looked at him questioningly.

"There's something that I've been meaning to give you," he said. "It might be somewhat overdue, but I hope that you will accept it all the same."

I carefully parted the ball and looked inside. Half was filled with a velvet pillow and tied on the pillow was Micah's high school ring. Tears sprang to my eyes even as I laughed. I untied the ring and took it out of the ball.

"It's perfect," I said.

"I'm glad you like it," he said. "It might be a little bit big on you. Maybe you'd rather wear this one instead."

I looked up at him and saw that he was holding an intricate diamond ring in his hand.

"Micah..."

"Charlotte, I have loved you for so long, and I will never stop loving you. When my life flashed before my eyes I saw so many moments that you should have been a part of, and I don't want us to miss any of those moments moving forward. I want to share every single one of them with you. Now that I have you, I feel like I have found everything that I have ever wanted or needed in life, even if I didn't know what I was looking for. Will you marry me?"

"Yes," I breathed.

I wondered if he had even been able to hear me, but his face lit up and he leaned down to kiss me. My hands shook as he slipped the ring onto my finger and I looked up into his eyes. Those eyes. Eyes that I hadn't been able to forget, and that I never had to for the rest of my life.

I hadn't planned on seeing my parents for Christmas, but the next day I couldn't resist going to their house. I needed them to see that I was still here. I had gotten through it and I was moving forward stronger and better. Micah had offered to go with me, but this was something that I needed to do myself. I promised that I wouldn't be gone long and made the slow, gradual drive down the mountain to their house. Both seemed stunned to see me, but I saw a flicker of happiness in my father's eyes and I couldn't help but feel compassion for him. There was obvious tension and division between my parents now and the future seemed uncertain. My mother had finally admitted that she had over-exaggerated my father's illness when I hadn't shown back up the day that she told me to. She knew that if I thought that he was sick and in any danger because of his heart, I would have to come home. Though she had scoffed and tried to brush it off, it turned out that she had believed me when I told her that there was a man who loved me and who I loved desperately, and it threatened her plans for my future. Her hope was that once I was back, I would begin to forget about my time on the mountain. She hoped that once I was back in my normal life I would remember everything that I had going for me, or at least everything that she thought that I had going for me, and I wouldn't be so inclined to want to be with Micah. My father said that he forgave her, but I could see the anger and distrust when he looked at her and I wondered if things would ever be the same between them again.

I didn't want to think about that now, though. It was Christmas and I had something truly incredible to tell them. We sat down in the parlor, flanking a Christmas tree decorated purely in white, and I decided there was no reason to delay it any longer.

"I came here today because I wanted to tell you that I'm engaged," I said.

Their eyes widened and both of them stared at me for a few long seconds as though they thought I might be joking, but I held my hand out to them to show them the ring that Micah had given me. He had it custom designed for me, and crafted featuring two small diamonds that had once been in jewelry worn by his mother and grandmother. It was exquisite, everything that I ever could have wanted in an engagement ring. There were still moments when I caught myself staring at it, tilting my hand back and forth so the stones would catch the light. It had been less than twenty-four hours since he proposed, but I wondered if my amazement if the beauty of the ring and the deep meaning that it carried would ever dissipate.

"You're engaged?" my father asked.

"To Micah?" my mother asked.

I looked at her, trying to keep the bitterness out of my expression. This was too joyful a day for me to think about anger or sadness. I wanted to put all of that behind me and just move forward. I nodded.

"Of course," I said. "Who else?"

They didn't say anything else and I stood. I wasn't sure if that had gone better or worse than I had hoped. They hadn't yelled or said anything scathing about him. But they also hadn't really reacted at all.

"You could have at least congratulated me," I said.

I started for the door but then I heard my mother's voice calling after me.

"Charlotte, there's something that I want to say to you."

I stopped and turned around.

"What is it?"

"I wanted to tell you that I'm sorry."

I was stunned by the sincerity and emotion in her voice. I took a few steps toward her again.

"You are?" I asked.

"Yes," she said. "I am so sorry that I never believed you about Daniel. I am so sorry that I never listened to you when you tried to tell me, and that I pushed you so hard to be with him. I should have been there for you. I should have protected you, not encouraged you to be in that situation. Is there any way that you could forgive me?"

I felt at a total loss for words. There's been so many times when I had hoped for this moment. I had prayed that they would understand what I had been going through and what it done to me, for them to push me to be with Daniel for so long. I had wanted them to acknowledge what this had caused and to apologize. Now that it happened, though, I didn't know how to process it. The more I thought about it, the more I realized that forgiving them was not what I needed to move forward. I needed to forgive myself.

"You didn't cause what he did to me," I said. "But you could have protected me. Thank you for saying that. You have no idea how much it means to me to hear you apologize. But I want you to know that I'm not carrying that with me any more. It doesn't matter. There's nothing that any of us can do about it and I, for one, don't want to go through the rest of my life hurting because of him. I feel like I've already given him enough of my time and my energy. I want the rest of it to be mine. And Micah's."

There was a strange, tense moment where it seemed that we didn't know what to say or do. My mother broke it by coming over and drawing me into a tight hug. When she stepped back, she was smiling. She lifted up my hand and admired my ring for a few seconds.

"Do you have any wedding plans yet?"

I spent the next hour with them talking about my ideas for the wedding and promising to consider some of theirs as well. I didn't want to be away from Micah too long, though, so I promised that we would both come back soon to have dinner with them. I was optimistic that they both seemed open to the possibility of meeting him again and starting over fresh. As I drove back up the mountain I thought about what I had said to my mother. I told her that I needed to forgive myself. I realized that this was completely true. I needed to come to terms with the decisions that I had made. I needed to forgive myself for falling under Daniel's manipulation to begin with. I needed to forgive myself for not recognizing what he was doing to me and for staying for as long as I did. I knew that I had finally gotten to a point in my life where I didn't need, or even really want, the approval of my parents. I didn't feel the guilt or the sadness that had come with the thought that I had disappointed them, or that I wasn't doing enough for them. I was ready to live my own life, and that meant that I no longer had to be a part of the social circle that has meant so much to them. That wasn't my world anymore. Maybe it never had been. All that mattered now was the world that I was going to share with Micah. I was going to go up onto the mountain and create my life there with him, though I did intend on luring him down more frequently than he usually went. There was still so much that we hadn't done together, and I wanted to make up for it all. I wanted to fill my mind with so many memories that I could feel as though I couldn't possibly lose them again.

When I got back to the lodge he was resting on the couch. Scout was chewing on one of the new toys that we had gotten for him for Christmas and there was a sense of peace and contentment in the air. I curled into the very corner of the couch and watch him sleep for a few moments. I was thankful that he seemed to be in less pain and the doctors had reassured us that, while it might take some time for him to heal completely, he would eventually, and there would be no lasting effects from either wound. I leaned over and kissed him on his cheek. His eyes slid open and he looked at me.

"Merry Christmas," I said.

"Merry Christmas," he said.

"What do you think about a beach wedding?" I asked.

He laughed.

"That certainly would be a change of venue," he said. "But that might be nice. At least we would know that we weren't going to get snowed in together again."

"I wouldn't mind being snowed in with you."

I smiled. I knew that Micah and I had different perspectives. There was nothing that was going to change that. We would always see the world in different ways, have different pasts, and have different things that brought us to where we were. But we could teach each other from those perspectives and learn from one another. But what I was looking forward to most was ignoring those perspectives and just living and loving one another.

THE END

61432872R00158

Made in the USA
Middletown, DE
10 January 2018